"I knew something was very wrong . . ."

"So I gently slid my screen open," my mother continued. "And God Almighty . . . there was this man with his arm stretched through the window on this side, holding a gun against Father Blake's temple . . ."

"Then?" Ben prompted.

"I screamed!" Mom's pale face went stark white. I wanted to stop Ben's questions. But Mom moved on. "I think I heard a muffled shot . . . Father Blake fell forward. Blood . . . there didn't seem to be much blood . . ."

"Did you get a good look at the killer?" Ben held my mother's hand.

"Yes. He had a cap pulled down over his brows, and it's dark in the confessional booth, so I didn't see much of his face. Definitely a man, slim, in black clothes."

"And did he see you?" Ben leaned forward.

"Yes! He shouted 'Rotten bitch!' That's when I ran out of the booth, up onto the altar, and into the sacristy, knocking poor Father Newell to his knees!"

Christ! The killer had seen my mother!

Don't miss these Jake O'Hara
Ghostwriter mysteries . . .

GHOSTWRITER
DEATH COMES FOR THE CRITIC
DEATH NEVER TAKES A HOLIDAY

MORE MYSTERIES FROM THE
BERKLEY PUBLISHING GROUP...

THE HERON CARVIC MISS SEETON MYSTERIES: Retired art teacher Miss Seeton steps in where Scotland Yard stumbles. "A most beguiling protagonist!" —*The New York Times*

by Heron Carvic
MISS SEETON SINGS
MISS SEETON DRAWS THE LINE
WITCH MISS SEETON
PICTURE MISS SEETON
ODDS ON MISS SEETON

by Hampton Charles
ADVANTAGE MISS SEETON
MISS SEETON AT THE HELM
MISS SEETON, BY APPOINTMENT

by Hamilton Crane
HANDS UP, MISS SEETON
MISS SEETON CRACKS THE CASE

MISS SEETON PAINTS THE TOWN
MISS SEETON BY MOONLIGHT
MISS SEETON ROCKS THE CRADLE
MISS SEETON GOES TO BAT
MISS SEETON PLANTS SUSPICION
STARRING MISS SEETON
MISS SEETON UNDERCOVER
MISS SEETON RULES
SOLD TO MISS SEETON
SWEET MISS SEETON
BONJOUR, MISS SEETON
MISS SEETON'S FINEST HOUR

KATE SHUGAK MYSTERIES: A former DA solves crimes in the far Alaska north...

by Dana Stabenow
A COLD DAY FOR MURDER
DEAD IN THE WATER
A FATAL THAW
BREAKUP

A COLD-BLOODED BUSINESS
PLAY WITH FIRE
BLOOD WILL TELL
KILLING GROUNDS
HUNTER'S MOON

CASS JAMESON MYSTERIES: Lawyer Cass Jameson seeks justice in the criminal courts of New York City in this highly acclaimed series... "A witty, gritty heroine."
—*New York Post*

by Carolyn Wheat
FRESH KILLS
MEAN STREAK
TROUBLED WATERS

DEAD MAN'S THOUGHTS
WHERE NOBODY DIES
SWORN TO DEFEND

JACK McMORROW MYSTERIES: The highly acclaimed series set in a Maine mill town and starring a newspaperman with a knack for crime solving... "Gerry Boyle is the genuine article." —Robert B. Parker

by Gerry Boyle
DEADLINE
LIFELINE
BORDERLINE

BLOODLINE
POTSHOT
COVER STORY

Remembrance of Murders Past

Noreen Wald

BERKLEY PRIME CRIME, NEW YORK

REMEMBRANCE OF MURDERS PAST

A Berkley Prime Crime Book / published by arrangement with the author

PRINTING HISTORY
Berkley Prime Crime mass-market edition / September 2001

Visit our website at
www.penguinputnam.com

ISBN: 0-425-18185-5

Berkley Prime Crime Books are published by The Berkley Publishing Group, a division of Penguin Putnam Inc., 375 Hudson Street, New York, New York 10014. The name BERKLEY PRIME CRIME and the BERKLEY PRIME CRIME design are trademarks belonging to Penguin Putnam Inc.

PRINTED IN THE UNITED STATES OF AMERICA

10 9 8 7 6 5 4 3 2 1

In loving memory of my parents,
Nora and Bill Feeley

Acknowledgments

Thanks to Susan Kavanagh and Betty Maclusky for reading, editing, and critiquing the manuscript. Thanks to Tom Johnson for the "second story" rappel work. Thanks to Paul Stuart, a Georgetown alum, for the history lesson. Thanks to Darrell Zimmerman for the Georgetown geography lesson. Thanks to Diane Dufour, Barbara Giorgio, Doris Holland, and Billy Reckdenwald, for listening to my plot points. Thanks to Joyce Sweeney and her class for their critique of chapter one. Finally, thanks to my agent, Peter Rubie, and my editor, Tom Colgan.

One

"His penance must have been Hell!" My mother said, referring to the killer she'd just confronted in St. Thomas More's church. "Jake, I can't believe Father Blake is dead. God! Murdered in the confessional!"

Mom had witnessed the shooter in action. Less than an hour ago. Now, sitting in our cheerful beige and white, super neat, cleaner than an autoclave Carnegie Hill kitchen, I thought, It's no wonder she can't believe it!

"Go on, Mom," I said.

"I'd arrived at six, just as confessions were ending. The church appeared empty, but Father Blake's light was still on, so I slipped into the penitent's seat on the left side and waited for Father to slide open the screen." Mom's always expertly applied mascara had stained her cheeks and her ash-blonde Diane Sawyer haircut had gone askew, resulting in a Dennis the Menace–style cowlick. She sighed, then wiped her eyes. "He was my favorite confessor and now . . ."

"Here." I handed her a cup of tea. "Take a sip; you'll feel better." Tea has been the O'Hara family's panacea since long before my ancestors sailed from Ireland and landed in New York.

"I didn't realize there was anyone on the other side of the booth and I wondered if he'd left, forgetting to turn off his light." I could hear the hysteria in my mother's voice. "But Father Blake shouted, 'My God, so this is the way it will end!' And I realized that he'd been listening to someone's confession."

Ben Rubin, Chief of Detectives at New York City's Nineteenth Precinct and my on again/off again boyfriend—at the moment, off, but since I haven't told him, I guess he doesn't know that—said, "Maura, what happened next? Did the priest say anything else? And the killer? What did he say? From what you're telling us, they may have known each other."

Totally complicating my so-called love life, my mother had just become engaged to Aaron Rubin, a retired New York City District Attorney, a current candidate for the United States Senate, and Ben's father. Tonight, looking at Ben's handsome face, his dark eyes filled with concern, I thought, Maybe I should rethink my split decision. As always, I didn't know what or who I really wanted. But I decided this was not the time to let my fickle heart interrupt my brain's concentration.

"Ben, it was so strange." Mom started weeping, then moaned as she tried to pull herself together again. "Father Blake—he sounded terrified—started to say, 'Bless me, Father, for I have sinned' . . . and I thought . . ."

"He'd made an act of contrition, Ben," I explained. "A penitent recites that to the priest, not the other way around."

"I knew something was very wrong," my mother continued, "so I gently slid my screen open . . . and God

Almighty . . . there was this man with his arm stretched through the window on his side, holding a gun against Father Blake's temple . . ."

"Then?" Ben prompted.

"I screamed!" Mom's pale face went stark white. I wanted to stop Ben's questions and put her to bed. Our old friend, Dr. Carter, was on his way over. But Mom moved on. "I think I heard a muffled shot . . . Father Blake fell forward. Blood . . . there didn't seem to be much blood . . . it stained his collar. He hardly ever wore his collar, you know . . ."

"Did you get a look at the killer?" Ben held my mother's hand.

"Yes. He had a cap pulled down over his brows and it's dark in the confessional booth, so I didn't see much of his face. Definitely a man, slim, in black clothes."

"And did he see you?" Ben leaned forward.

"Yes! He shouted 'Rotten bitch!' That's when I ran out of the booth, up onto the altar, and into the sacristy, knocking poor Father Newell to his knees!"

Christ! The killer had seen my mother!

"You know, Ben," she said, "there was something rather odd about the killer's voice."

"How so?"

"Well, he could have been your typical movie hit man, dressed all in black, with that hat covering his hair and the top of his face—but his voice sounded cultured, even though he was shouting."

"Did he follow you?" Ben asked.

"I don't know, Ben." My mother shook her head. "I never looked back. Father Newell and I dashed out the side door and into the rectory, where he dialed 911. Then I called Jake." She stood, turned to me, and smiled. Weak, but warm. "Jake, you must have broken the record for running from 92nd Street to 89th Street. With all those crowds of people on Madison Avenue, coming home from work, I hope you didn't injure any innocent pedestrians!"

"That's okay, Mom." I slipped an arm around her slim waist. "This book I'm ghosting is so damn dull that I welcomed the opportunity to get a little exercise."

. . . . .

Dr. Carter left, after giving Mom a sedative which she had refused to swallow in favor of a martini, and Ben went back to homicide, after giving me a chaste kiss on the cheek. Maybe he'd lost interest in me!

Gypsy Rose Liebowitz, who'd dashed out of a Deepak Chopra signing at her New Age bookstore when I called, had arrived. She stood at the stove, dressed in her Charles Jourdan pumps and her coral pink Chanel suit that, rather than clashing, looked great with her mass of curly red hair, deftly cracking eggs into a white bowl, while she, Mom, and I attempted to put the pieces of the mystery together.

My mother's longtime best friend and Carnegie Hill's favorite fortune-teller, she possessed psychic abilities that frequently matched her cooking skills. Gypsy Rose whipped those eggs with a vengeance, adding sun-dried tomatoes and finely chopped bits of parsley, then placed homemade biscuits into the toaster oven to warm.

I'd have preferred to see Mom in bed, following doctor's orders, but I knew she'd never rest when she said, "*My* closest friend and *my* only daughter can't work on *my* murder without *my* input!" So I agreed to mix her a martini.

Father Billy Blake had been the most charming and controversial priest in the Archdiocese of New York. An anti–death penalty activist, in addition to his duties at St. Thomas More's, Blake had been serving as spiritual advisor to the Metropolitan Correction Center's current criminal-of-the-century resident. Notorious hit man Nick Amas would be transported, later this month, from the center to the Terra Haute, Indiana, Federal Penitentiary's death row. He'd been convicted for three highly publicized and particularly cold-blooded drug-related murders. Amas had cut out his victims' tongues and sliced off their ears and noses, before putting a bullet through their brains. Then he'd sent the spare body parts to the United States Attorney. Shipped them. Collect.

After a six-week federal task force's nationwide search, he'd been arrested in a whorehouse in Las Vegas, tried, and convicted. Mom and Gypsy Rose had followed the trial on Court TV. And only yesterday, Nick Amas, supposedly, had made what could be his last confession to Billy Blake. A Mexican drug cartel, the Office of the United States Attorney, and most New Yorkers were really curious about the content of that confession.

"So," Gypsy Rose said, "do you think Father Blake's murder is connected to Nick Amas?"

"It would seem likely. A bullet in the head. Hit man–style." I finished my fourth cup of tea. "Maybe the shooter believed that Nick had told Father Blake something—"

"That would incriminate another criminal," my mother broke in. "A fellow murderer or . . ."

Gypsy Rose stopped scrambling and spun around to face us. Her green eyes filled with anger. "Or something to land that drug lord in jail! You know, the biggie, Senor Cali, the one the Feds can't seem to get enough evidence on to indict!"

"The seal of the confessional can't be broken," my mother said.

"That's true." I nodded. "But the killer may not be up on canon law."

Mom frowned. "Well, Jake, that eliminates Cali. He may be a drug czar and the head of Mexico's most murderous cartel, but he is a practicing Catholic. Never misses Sunday mass. I read that in *People*. Cali would know about a priest's vow of silence!"

There was no arguing with her logic.

Gypsy Rose placed plates of steaming eggs in front of us. Along with the biscuits and her strawberry jam. I knew the taste would equal or surpass the presentation. "You need strength. Eat, Maura," she ordered my mother who, to my surprise, picked up her fork and dug in.

"This is wonderful, Gypsy Rose!" I said, thinking how rubbery Mom's eggs always were. The O'Haras were not chefs. For sure.

"I'm going to ask Zelda to contact Father Blake's spirit guide," Gypsy Rose said as she sat down. "We need some answers and we need them fast!" I knew Gypsy Rose must be as terrified as I was that the killer would come after Mom. I also knew that Zelda Fitzgerald, one of Gypsy Rose's three personal spirit guides in the world beyond, had come through for us before.

"That will be great!" my mother said. "I'll feel ever so much better with Zelda on the case!"

As a ghostwriter, I've worked with some mighty strange clients. Totally way out there. Certifiable fruit-cakes. But none stranger than the two dear New York nuts who sat with me at the kitchen table, contemplating a chat with the dead. God! Had I become as weird as they were?

TWO

At eight o'clock, Mom and Gypsy Rose settled down to watch one of their all-time favorite Katharine Hepburn videos. Knowing that Aaron Rubin had just hopped off the Washington shuttle, returning from his meeting with the senior Senator from New York, and was on his way here from La Guardia, I figured it would be okay for me to disappear for a while. With questions reeling round my mind, I wanted to pick Dennis Kim's brain. Maybe that wasn't all I wanted from my childhood crush.

My mistake was switching on the ANN cable station before Mom popped *Summertime* into the VCR. Father Billy Blake's murder hadn't made any of the networks' 6:30 P.M. national news programs, but ANN interrupted anchor Wendy Wu's—an annoyingly attractive woman and Dennis Kim's ex-wife—exclusive Madonna and child interview to bring America the gory details of the celebrity priest's murder.

The entertainment corner in Mom's big, old, high-

ceiling bedroom included two cream and white striped
club chairs with ottomans, a round table with a reading
lamp, and two tall bookcases. A large, white wicker ar-
moire housed a television, a VCR, many tapes of old
movies—filed by decade—a CD player, and a small
selection of discs. Sinatra, Bennett, Fred Astaire, Rose-
mary Clooney, and Johnny Ray. Except for a few show
tunes, my mother had no music more recent than 1960.

I'd grown up listening to my maternal grandparents'
records from World War II. I still prefer jazz and the
old standards like "As Time Goes By" and "I'll Be Seeing You" to the top forty, though I did drag Mom and
Gypsy Rose to see *Tommy* on Broadway. They loved it;
Gypsy Rose even went so far as to compare the rock
opera to *Madam Butterfly*.

A few months ago, I'd cajoled Too Tall Tom, my best
friend and a fellow ghost—late in the craze—to take a
series of Lindy Hop lessons. The beat that I'd danced to
so many years ago, when Mom and I jitterbugged
around the apartment, lived on in the 86th Street ballroom!

Wendy Wu's hyped-up, rapid-fire reportage swept
away those stardust memories, and a panic attack, sharp
as pellets, ripped through my gut when Wendy announced, in her best Bette Davis voice of doom imita-
tion, "An unidentified witness has described the
gunman."

"That's not true!" Gypsy Rose jumped off the ottoman
and shouted at the screen. "The *witness* saw nothing!"

"I certainly couldn't pick him out in a lineup." Mom
sank back into her chair. "Oh God! Of course, the killer
doesn't know that!"

Gypsy Rose and I stared at each other. Wendy Wu's
dramatic presentation continued. "ANN's sources have
confirmed that the New York City Police Department

will be working in close cooperation with Gregory Ford, from the United States Attorney's Office."

Jesus! That woman had just issued an open invitation for the drug cartel to put out a contract on my mother!

The downstairs buzzer signaled Aaron Rubin's arrival. I dialed Dennis.

. . . . .

Fifteen minutes later, I sat next to Dennis Kim, inhaling the delicious scent of the leather in his cream color Rolls Royce convertible as we drove down Fifth Avenue, going nowhere.

With the top down, the sights, smells, and sounds of the city's prettiest avenue competed for my attention. I love New York in June and this early summer evening was so delicious. And the sky so full of stars. Many of Carnegie Hill's residents were out for a stroll. Kids, seniors, joggers, grande dames, Rollerbladers, politicians, and actors. I spotted our neighbor Woody Allen, shoulders hunched and hands jammed into his windbreaker's pockets, as if he were freezing in the seventy-degree night air. There was no problem separating the locals from the tourists. Plenty of the latter on the town tonight; they loved New York in June, too. But only to visit.

At 86th Street, Dennis pulled over and bought two hot, salted pretzels and two Diet Cokes from a sidewalk vendor in front of the entrance to Central Park. The last of the big spenders.

"Let me guess why you called," he said. "Sounded like serious stuff. Are you finally ready to fire that sad sack agent of yours, Sam Kelley, and hire an entertainment attorney who will earn his fifteen percent? Or, better yet, are you finally ready to tell me that you love me?"

I felt my toes heat up. His presence has ignited my feet for over a quarter of a century. At the age of eight and the new kid on the block, I'd tried to crash an all-boys street hockey game and had taken a bite out of the hand that held me back. Dennis Kim's.

My heart may have been wavering about him all these years, but the tingles in my toes had remained constant. Even not acting as my agent, Dennis has tried to advance my ghostwriting career, but some disaster or death always seemed to terminate my assignments. Much as I yearned to write my own mystery novel, with my own name on its cover, lack of money had kept me an anonymous ghost.

After my last cruise into murder's uncharted waters, I swore that in the future, my only dealings with death would occur on the pages of a manuscript. That same Charonesque voyage had brought Dennis and me to the edge of a real romance, and I'd promised myself that I'd straighten out my personal life.

Tonight I realized not only had I not changed either my professional or my personal life, both had become even bigger messes. Murder had popped up again, putting Mom's life in danger. And I, while totally incapable of commitment, still wanted two men.

"I guess you haven't heard. Father Billy Blake's been murdered and Mom was an eyewitness!"

"Christ!" Dennis swerved to the left and some of my soda splashed on the front seat. "Tell me exactly what happened."

By the time he made a right on Madison, heading back uptown, I'd hit the highlights. "Where are we going, Dennis?" We'd passed 90th Street.

"Back to your co-op. I have to speak to Maura."

"Why? Talk to me. I'll tell her whatever it is." I would have preferred not having my prospective stepfather,

Aaron Rubin, and his son's competition, Dennis Kim, under the same roof. Not tonight.

"No, Jake, I need to tell her myself." He double-parked in front of his father's fruit stand on the corner of 92nd and Madison.

．．．．．

Katharine Hepburn and Rossano Brazzi were sharing a kiss, but no one was watching. Dennis Kim's announcement captured Mom's, Gypsy Rose's, and Aaron's complete attention. "Billy Blake hired me yesterday to represent him in a seven-figure book deal. His memoirs reveal death row confidences—though not the convicts' confessions—and include two tell-all chapters about the Mexican mob. The book is scheduled to be published on the day that Nick Amas is transferred to Terra Haute's death row!"

Gypsy Rose gasped, "Surely, Father Blake knew that by signing that contract, he'd signed his own death warrant!"

Aaron Rubin nodded. "That's right, Dennis, why would Blake do such a thing?"

"He asked me to arrange for half the advance and all his royalties to be given to Amnesty International. With the balance—a hefty sum—Blake could have a new life and a new identity."

"Won't the book deal leak out?" I asked. A swell of music came from the VCR and my eyes wandered over for a second to St. Mark's Square. "Why would Father Blake have put his life in jeopardy? Even if he actually planned on leaving the priesthood? Which I doubt. Literary types love to brag about potential bestsellers. No way would they have been able to keep a hot ticket like that a secret!"

Dennis shook his head. "I've been assured that only

the editor and I know what the book's really about. And I haven't read it. I advised Blake against the project, but it was too late, I'd come aboard after he'd cut the deal."

Mom had said nothing; she'd just stared at Dennis. Now she walked over and put her hands on his shoulders. Her green eyes looking up into his gold-flecked ones. "I've known you well for a very long time. You're trying to protect me. There's something else isn't there? What aren't you telling us?"

Dennis sighed and hugged my mother. "You always were too smart for me, Maura. I had a phone call earlier today from Maggie Roth, she's Blake's editor's assistant. Don Taylor—that's the editor—left work early on Friday afternoon, and his wife says he never arrived home. Maggie scoured the office today, looking for Blake's manuscript. But it seems to have disappeared along with his editor."

Three

I crawled out of bed Sunday morning, groggy from lack of sleep and puzzled by the dream that I had just before waking. A handsome young man, a good ten or twelve years younger than I, with smooth olive skin and the flattest stomach I've ever seen—asleep or awake—had been kissing my toes and working his way up my leg. Though I didn't recognize him, this fine specimen's excellent technique felt vaguely familiar. I really wanted to roll over and go back to sleep, but I could hear Mom and Gypsy Rose rattling around the apartment.

Despite my best efforts to talk them out of it last night, the ladies had insisted that we go ahead with our plans for Sunday. So, of course, Dennis and Aaron then had insisted on accompanying us. Well, isn't this just great? Dennis and I were practically double-dating with Ben's father and my mother. How the hell do I get myself into . . .

"Jake!" My mother's shout startled me. "Hurry up, darling! Emmie's memorial mass is at ten-thirty. And

you'll want a nice cup of tea before we leave." I could
smell the bagels burning. Obviously Mom, not Gypsy
Rose, had made breakfast. "We don't want to be late.
Shake a leg!"

I shook my left leg—the one that the handsome young
stranger had been kissing in dreamland—and hopped in
the shower.

A memorial mass and a visit to Calvary Cemetery on
this sunny morning after Mom's close encounter with
murder struck me as a bit eerie; however, I really wanted
to go, too. Exactly a year ago, my best friend and sister
ghostwriter had been murdered. Emily Brontë Rogers
and I had been baptized and had started first grade together at St. Joan of Arc's in Jackson Heights. When
my mother and I had moved from Queens to Manhattan
after Mom's great-aunt died and left her wonderful, old-
world co-op to her favorite grandniece, we'd remained
close friends with the Rogers family.

Em's death had been tough on all of us. Mom, Gypsy
Rose, Ivan (her crazy Hungarian boyfriend), the other
ghosts, and I still missed her laughter, loyalty, and flair
for high drama. But for the Rogers family, especially
Emmie's dad, mourning the death of their only daughter
had become an obsession. No way would Mom and I
have missed her memorial. Since the anniversary of Emmie's death fell on a Sunday, her father had gone to
great lengths, obtaining special permission to hold the
service this morning!

Shivering under a cold rinse—that some sadist of a
hair stylist had prescribed as mandatory to stimulate my
scalp—I told myself that a trip to Calvary might take
Mom's mind off Father Blake's murder. Right, Jake, a
cemetery's the perfect place to forget *about the dead*.

I wrapped a towel around my head, applied some
blush, lipstick, eye shadow, and mascara, thinking I was

beginning to look like my mother. When I'd turned thirty-four last month, I admitted that I had too much gray to be called streaks and, wanting to stay blonde, began to use the same shade of Clairol as she did. I dried my Winter Wheat hair, threw on a navy blue shift and sandals, and headed for the kitchen to breakfast on a burnt bagel.

My mother was on the phone, staring out the window as she listened. She appeared to have recovered from Saturday evening's ordeal. Both women looked ready to roll. Mom wore a big straw hat and a double-breasted taupe blazer with matching pleated skirt and pumps. Gypsy Rose, dressed this morning in a smart black linen pants suit, served me a perfectly toasted English muffin, strawberry jam, fresh grapefruit juice, and tea in a small pot covered with a brown and beige plaid cozy. She winked, then gestured to the garbage where three totally cremated bagels had gone to their well-deserved final resting place. Thank God someone had called Mom, and Gypsy Rose had seized the opportunity to trash those suckers, or I might have been forced to swallow soot spread with cream cheese.

"You'll never guess who that was!" Mom hung up the phone, appearing flushed and not, I suspected, from an over-application of blush.

"Who?" Gypsy Rose and I asked as one.

"Clare Blake. Father Blake's younger sister. She just arrived from Washington this morning to make the funeral arrangements. Father Newell told her that I'd been with her brother in the confessional when he—well, when he died—and now she wants to talk to me."

"Jesus!" I almost choked on my muffin. "What the hell is wrong with Father Newell? No one is supposed to know who witnessed Blake's murder!"

"Ben will be furious." Gypsy Rose shook her head, causing her curls to tumble into her eyes.

"Why do we have to tell him?" Mom shoved a saucer into the dishwasher. "Anyway, I invited her over here tonight. Around seven."

My mother was saved by the bell. Aaron and Dennis were waiting for us downstairs.

· · · · ·

Gypsy Rose, Mom, and I climbed into the backseat. Aaron was up front with Dennis. How cozy!

With surprisingly light traffic and Dennis's heavy foot on the gas pedal, we were on the Triborough Bridge in no time. Not wanting to discuss death—Father Billy's or anyone else's—I decided to talk politics. The governor had asked Aaron Rubin, a former DA and a brilliant legal mind, to run in a special election to fill an empty Senate seat. He was the odds-on favorite. When my mother married Ben's father, she'd be a Washington wife, at least part time. I didn't think I'd like that very much. Total pain that she is, I enjoy having her underfoot. And I couldn't remain in the co-op without sharing its monthly expenses. Mom had suggested that Aaron and she buy a second apartment, creating a duplex where all of us could live. However, even with two floors, and Aaron spending much of his time in D.C., I didn't want a stepfather in the house. If he lost the election, the situation would be even worse; he wouldn't be on Capitol Hill, he'd be in Carnegie Hill full-time.

"So, Aaron, what do the latest polls predict?" I asked. "Is Mr. Rubin going to Washington?"

"Sure looks that way, Jake. I'm thinking about buying a co-op in the Westchester. It's a grand old building near the National Cathedral, built circa 1929. Art deco architecture, wrought iron gates, and sunken gardens.

The apartment I'm interested in has two bedrooms and two baths, but they're enormous rooms. High ceilings, a solarium, and dentil molding. You'll love it!"

Gypsy Rose, scrunching up her nose, glanced at me, then said, "When's the wedding?"

Jesus, maybe death would have been a better topic of conversation.

Aaron craned his neck to give my mother a dazzling smile. "Can we tell them, Maura?"

My mother actually giggled. Love will do that to a sixty-something.

"In October, on Columbus Day. Then I'll be a part-time Washingtonian wife." She smiled at Aaron.

"Congratulations." I didn't smile. "Planning a big wedding?"

"Jake, darling," she said, "this will be a small affair. A mass at St. Thomas More's, followed by a party for a few friends, and then off to the Greek Isles. From there, we're sailing to Italy. Doesn't it sound divine?"

Columbus Day? When had all these "divine" decisions been made behind my back? I felt Gypsy Rose squeeze the fingers on my left hand.

Dennis said, "Do I get to give the bride away?"

. . . . .

I didn't say another word till we arrived in Jackson Heights. My four companions, however, taking on Martha Stewart's least attractive qualities, rambled on about wedding etiquette. I'd tuned out in Woodside, when they'd decided that Dennis and his father, Mr. Kim, a greengrocer, poet, and our longtime family friend, would escort Mom down the aisle.

The Jackson Heights of my mother's childhood was light years away from today's multicultural mini metropolis. The community resonated with the sounds of sitars and castanets. On 74th Street, women in saris and men in turbans ran shops whose wares spilled over onto the sidewalks, creating an open marketplace. We could have been in Bombay instead of Queens. Along 37th Avenue, between 70th and 81st Streets, restaurants offered tastes of India, Cuba, Korea, and China, and a wide selection from Central and South American countries. Their competing aromas were overwhelming so early in the morning.

The old guard, mostly elderly WASP women, wearing pastel suits circa 1955, were out in full force, walking to services at the Congregational and Episcopalian churches. Hispanic girls in their colorful summer dresses were heading for St. Joan's. The Irish and Italian senior citizens were going there, too.

The new minorities—all seventy-plus different varieties—had driven most of the older minorities, the Irish, Italians, Germans, Poles, Greeks, and Jews, to Long Island or New Jersey. A smattering of each of those ethnic groups had remained entrenched. People like Emmie's parents, who'd decided to hang in there with the new wave of immigrants, had never regretted it.

Filled with pockets of culture from around the world, Jackson Heights has been the subject of numerous newspaper articles and glossy magazine profiles, making it, like Grandma's porch furniture, both shabby chic and trendy. Manhattanites "discovered" its authentic ethnic restaurants, so now on weekends the locals have trouble eating out in their own neighborhood. And 74th Street has turned into the sari-shopping capital of America.

While Mom mourns her hometown's lost elegance and anonymity, I like the energy, seeing Jackson Heights's bustling multicultural businesses as a harbinger of what most of New York City's neighborhoods will be like in ten years.

. . . . .

Dennis pulled the Rolls into the pastor's parking spot in front of St. Joan's, and we all climbed the steps to the upper church. The organist played "Ava Maria," its strains filling the air and breaking my heart. My mother linked her arm through mine.

Four

We were joining the Rogers family in the first pew. On our way down the long aisle, I spotted several members of Ghostwriters Anonymous. A Too Tall Tom sighting came easy; even seated, he was head and shoulders above the crowd. I waved to him and Modesty. Jane, the early bird in my circle of close ghosts, had staked out a seat down front—on what would be the bride's side if this were a wedding.

A traditional and beautiful church, built over fifty years ago, St. Joan's is as large as the diocese's only cathedral in Brooklyn. The stained-glass windows glistened with sunshine as the congregation knelt in silent prayer, waiting for Emmie's memorial mass to begin.

I felt too nudgy to pray. Spooked by Em's murder and by Father Blake's. And by Joan of Arc, who'd been burned at the stake.

Legend has it that Joan's heart didn't burn, but what about the rest of her? What about those witches burned to death in Salem? Man's inhumanity to women. And how about Hell, where our souls could roast through eternity? Fire flickered through my head. I wiped my brow.

Gypsy Rose leaned over. "Is it too warm for you in here?"

. . . . .

After mass, twelve of Emmie's family and friends gathered for brunch at Armando's on 37th Avenue and 73rd Street, before visiting her grave at Calvary. This has been the Rogers and O'Hara families' favorite restaurant. For years and years. With all the trendy, ethnic choices that the neighborhood now offered, we still ate at Armando's. And why not? Though its decor reminded me of all the other Italian restaurants that I've eaten in, its food remained outstanding, including the best baked ziti I've ever tasted. Anywhere!

Jerry, the owner, and the wait staff, expecting our onslaught, had pushed three tables together, lengthwise, along the windows, under the glass dome in the outer dining room.

I wound up between Aaron and Dennis. Neither the family nor the ghostwriters had any idea that Mom had witnessed Father Blake's death, so those who did know were spared their barrage of questions and they were spared our concern about Maura O'Hara's safety.

But, as we dug into our chicken picatta or eggs Benedict, served with the best Italian bread in Queens, Billy Blake's murder seemed to be on everyone's mind.

Mike Rogers, his eyes red-rimmed, sat directly across the table from me. He buttered his bread and said, "That drug lord Cali must have ordered the hit, don't you think, Aaron?"

"A strong possibility, but not so easy to prove." Aaron poured a cup of coffee and passed the carafe to Gypsy

Rose on his right. Mom, in deep conversation with Linda Rogers at the other end of the table, appeared to be paying no attention to the men's exchange.

"Why?" Mike asked. "Isn't his motive the most obvious? Cali believes that Amas confessed all to Father Blake. I'll bet Amas won't live long enough to sit in the electric chair!"

"The Feds agree with your hypothesis," Aaron said. "Greg Ford, you know, the United States Attorney, told me this morning that Nick Amas's security is so tight he's been assigned his own round-the-clock guard."

I asked, "Are they planning on questioning Cali?"

"Get this; it's been reported that he's on a pilgrimage to visit Our Lady of Guadeloupe's shrine. Cali's sister has cancer. Pancreatic. He brought her there to pray for a miracle. A cure." Aaron shook his head. "But they've vanished. No one can locate either one of them."

"Well, there you are!" my mother shouted, turning all eyes in her direction. "Any man with such devotion to the Virgin Mary would know that Father Blake would never break the seal of the confessional! Therefore," she waved her napkin for emphasis, "Senor Cali would have no motive!"

Mom sounded like F. Lee Bailey defending the devil.

. . . . .

Losing a dear friend has left a huge hole in my life. Emmie and I would dash off to a movie on impulse rather than design, then devour hot fudge sundaes at Serendipity's more by design than impulse. On occasion, Too Tall Tom filled the void. And then some! I consider him my best friend, but he could never take Emmie's place. Nor could Modesty, our Ghostwriters Anonymous group's not-so-closeted misogynist, who, strangely, has become another close friend. Nor Jane, a successful how-to/self-help ghost. No one could.

People we love aren't replaced when they die; the best we can hope for is that we'll meet them again . . . in the world beyond, while waiting to be reincarnated, or, as I've been taught, up in Heaven. Fear of fire has led me to believe, as Mom does, that a hereafter in Hell is not an acceptable option. Gypsy Rose says we all travel through eternity in cliques. Meeting, and sometimes marrying, the same old souls The gal who'd been your pal in a previous life might be your husband in the next go-round.

. . . . .

Dennis drove through Calvary's high gates, with Modesty's old VW convertible, its top down, close on his tail. In the Beetle's backseat, Too Tall Tom's knees stuck straight up like chopsticks in a bowl of fried rice. Modesty had been bumper-to-bumper behind Dennis since we'd left Armando's, making all of us in the Rolls even edgier.

Actually, she'd never liked most men either. Dennis, "that decadent capitalist on parade," has become her favorite whipping boy.

When we stopped a few yards from Emmie's grave site, Modesty jumped out and slammed the car door. A petite woman, her pale red hair almost amber in the bright sunlight, her light eyes covered in Elton John–style sunglasses, and her fair skin turning pink, Modesty wore one of her many monk-like ankle-length tunics. Today's was chocolate brown and belted with her silver rosary bead belt. Coral-painted toes peeked out of her St. Francis of Assisi sandals. Ever since she'd fallen for the "reformed" cat-burglar-turned-author Rickie Romero, who was now her live-in lover, her long unsung femininity had been popping out in the damnedest places.

"Where the hell is Jane?" Modesty yelled toward the Rolls Royce passengers, as we began to exit the car. "She told me in the ladies room at Armando's that she had a ride; I assumed she meant with Dennis."

Too Tall Tom unfolded himself and crawled out of the bug. Stretching his legs, he said, "I think Jane's in a cab heading back to the city."

"Why?" I asked, then wished I hadn't.

"Because," Modesty shrieked, "that overpaid how-to ghost is afraid of cemeteries. She told me this morning that she's had it with death. And that we're all obsessed with it! Says hanging out at graves depresses her. Scares her silly. As if she wasn't Silly Putty to begin with! But I didn't believe her for a minute, I'll bet Ms. Label-Loving Jane has gone to Bloomingdale's!"

Emmie's grave sat on a hill in the old section of Calvary. While her tombstone was marble and modern, most of the others in this part of the cemetery were stone slabs from the nineteenth century. On the larger graves, entire family histories were listed, their carved names, birthdays, and dates of death often covering a hundred years or more. I'd brought my camera. Maybe Jane was right; maybe her fellow ghosts had turned into ghouls. But since my stint at *Manhattan Magazine*, I'd become quite the photojournalist. All these old crypts, topped with angels or saints and featuring pictures of those who were buried underneath all that Gothic glory, proved to be irresistible.

After saying a prayer to Emmie, asking her to look after my mother, I wandered off, shooting the surrounding graves, concentrating on the most ornate headstones and tombs. Some of the mausoleums could have housed a live family of five.

In the background, I could hear Mike Rogers leading Em's friends and family in the first decade of the glorious mysteries of the rosary. I stopped in front of a large stone slab, dark in color and rough around the edges, compelled to read the inscriptions.

Carved in deep, bold, and wide letters, THE SCANLON FAMILY was centered near the top of the stone. The first Scanlon to die had been a Clifford James, born August 22, 1812, County Cork, Ireland, died New York City, November 17, 1886. The next to go had been Clifford's beloved wife, Bridget, who'd outlived him by ten years. I rubbed my hand along the stone and, as if on a Ouija board, my fingers flew—unbidden—down the list of names. My heart raced and fear, not unlike that lifelong fear of fire, clutched at my throat. I sank to my knees as my fingers traced the last name on the stone.

Karen Scanlon, born in New York City, February 13, 1948, died in Washington, D.C., May 23, 1967. Only nineteen years old! And she'd died on the day I'd been born!

Long, thick dark hair spread out on a pillow flashed through my head. A young man's flat, firm stomach, moving in perfect harmony above a slim body. Hips lifting to match his pace. A hand reaching for an Oxford-cloth blue shirt. A pop, then pain . . . head hurting so much . . . bright red blood seeping across the rumpled white sheets.

I screamed.

Mom, Gypsy Rose, and Modesty had surrounded me when I opened my eyes.

"What happened, Jake, did you faint?" Modesty helped me to my feet.

"I don't know. Maybe. I never have before, so I'm not sure."

Gypsy Rose stared at me, her gaze so intense I wondered if she could see into my mind. "Are you okay, Jake? Did you have a . . ."

"A what?" my mother cried.

"Nothing, Mom, I'm fine."

Though I suspected that Gypsy Rose smelled ESP in action here, there was no way I could explain this experience!

I knew how the girl in the grave had died. I'd felt her pain!

Five

Timmy Rogers, the youngest of Mike and Linda's three sons, came up behind me as I started for the car, just as he had done on the day of Emmie's funeral. Considered a nerd by his older jock brothers, Timmy has always been Mom's and my favorite. He'd just finished his first year at NYU Law School. "Fourth in his class!" Mom had told me, sounding as proud as if he had been her own son.

"I saw you at the Scanlon grave." Timmy gestured over his shoulder, toward the headstone.

I disentangled myself from Modesty's strong grip on my right arm. "Go on ahead, Modesty. Tell Mom I'll be right there." Then I gave Timmy my full attention.

"Do you know something about the Scanlon family?"

He shrugged. "It's just that when I visit Emmie—I still come about once a week, you know—anyway, lots of times, there's this guy standing in front of their grave. Arrives in a limo. Then he just stands there and stares at the tomb, while the driver waits. Never even glances my way, never kneels to say a prayer. Never stays more than a few minutes. And he always leaves a dozen roses. Blood red ones."

"What does this guy look like?"

"Hispanic. Middle age, but in good shape. Looks like he works out. Great threads. Armani. Dresses like Regis on that millionaire show that Mom's after me to try out for." With his attention to details, Timmy would make a great trial lawyer—or contestant.

"Anything else?"

"Why are you so interested in all this? Don't you have enough mystery in your life?"

I started, then lost my balance.

Timmy steadied my arm. "Are you okay?"

"Yes. I wonder if that guy's visiting Karen Scanlon. She died thirty-four years ago. On my birthday."

"Good Lord, no wonder you're shaky. That's weird, isn't it?"

I nodded. "Go on."

"Well, basically, that's it. As I say, the guy never looked my way." Timmy, still holding my arm, started walking toward the cars. "It's been a long time since we've gone to Rathbone's. I'll come to New York one Sunday and we'll have dinner. Okay?"

"Wonderful! I'd like that, Timmy."

Funny. People from Jackson Heights always referred to the borough of Manhattan as New York, or the City, forgetting that Queens was part of New York City, too.

"Hurry up, Jake!" Modesty yelled. "Your cell phone is ringing!"

I listened to Jane explain how the big brunch had upset her stomach, so she'd grabbed a cab back to the city and, feeling somewhat better, had the driver drop her off at Bloomingdale's.

"I had to use the ladies room, Jake! You know how

urgent that can be! I'd have never made it home. But, since I was here, anyway, I thought I'd take a peek at the Ellen Tracy summer sale. Would you believe the fall collection is being previewed already?"

I chuckled, then handed the phone to Modesty. She'd called that one right. Jane deserved to engage in dialogue with her worse critic.

But Modesty simply snarled, "Philistine," pushed the off button, handed the phone to me, and stomped back to her VW. Too Tall Tom, twisted like a large sourdough pretzel in the Bug's backseat, awaited her.

I climbed into the Rolls next to Mom, and Dennis sailed through the cemetery gates, heading for the 59th Street Bridge, taking us home to Manhattan.

"Are you okay, Jake?" My mother asked. "Good Lord, you almost passed out at that old grave!"

Gypsy Rose said, "You dropped your camera. I have it in my bag. You gave us quite a scare, darling!" Her tote held all sorts of treasures. Even on short jaunts, Gypsy Rose traveled equipped for any emergency. So did Mom, who never left home without tissues, breath spray, and mascara, among sundry other items.

"I'm fine, ladies, just felt a little queasy back there." I smiled. "Worry about Jane. The total cost of her shopping spree will include dealing with Modesty's wrath. That's too high a price for anyone to have to pay!"

"I spoke to Ben this morning. He thinks that Blake's death and his editor's disappearance could be connected." Dennis had switched gears, turning the conversation back to Father Blake's murder; I almost felt grateful. Karen Scanlon haunted me and I didn't want Mom and Gypsy Rose to know that.

"Is Ben investigating how the editor vanished?" I asked.

"He is," Aaron answered, "and so is Greg Ford's office. "Seems neither my son nor the Attorney General believes in coincidences."

"So the editor might have been murdered, too." Gypsy Rose shuddered. Since the afternoon sun had warmed up the cream color leather in Dennis's convertible, she certainly wasn't cold.

"Aaron, do you really think that Cali's behind it?" I asked. "That he ordered a hit to silence Father Billy?"

He turned around to face us, placing a hand on the back of his seat. "While I'd never refute your mother's amazing knowledge and understanding of her faith and its doctrine, I know that Cali, a self-proclaimed practicing Catholic, is also an international drug lord and mass murderer, who may not share Maura's unwavering belief in the seal of the confessional. He may well have been worried that Blake would blab. So, yes, I do suspect him. However, there are other candidates."

"Who?" My headache had returned with a vengeance. I rummaged through Mom's bag-of-tricks for the Tylenol.

"Father Billy administered the last rites to at least a dozen condemned men," Aaron said. "All across the country. Some of those recent executions have been high profile. You run into lots of unsavory chaps on death row. Could be that one of Blake's former penitents confessed more than his own sins. And could be that one of his associates has been concerned about that final confession. Concerned enough to seal Father Blake's lips permanently."

Dennis said, "Right. Then there's another angle to consider. Coming at it from the other side."

My mother snatched her bag from me and, without even inquiring as to what I'd been searching for, stuck her hand into its depths and came up with a small bottle of Tylenol.

As I struggled to open it, Gypsy Rose asked, "What angle?"

"There are lots of pro–death penalty advocates who have gone over the line," Dennis said. "They think the Billy Blakes of this world, who are working to abolish the death penalty, are agents of Satan. One of them could have killed him. To shut him up. In this case, to stop him from spreading his message."

"Isn't that too far-fetched?" Gypsy Rose asked. "Way out there in Loony Tunes land?"

Since I knew that was the land where Dennis thought Gypsy Rose resided, I stifled a laugh. Then I pulled opened the mini bar and poured a glass of water to wash down my pills.

"What about the antiabortion activists who've bombed the clinics?" Dennis asked Gypsy Rose. "Would this be so different?"

He then made a right onto First Avenue, heading north.

My cell phone's sharp ring interrupted her response.

Ben said, "There's no easy way to say this, Jake. Please bring your mother down to the Nineteenth Precinct now."

"Why?" I almost choked on the word.

Mom and Gypsy Rose were scrutinizing me and, in these close quarters, I had nowhere to hide. I tried to smile.

"We found Father Blake's editor. In a garbage dump in New Jersey. Shot through the head, execution-style. The same caliber bullet that killed Father Blake. Probably from the same gun."

"Why do you want Mom?"

"One of Cali's lieutenants could be our man. He's a suspect in another hit. Same MO. I want your mother to look at him in a lineup."

"But she didn't see anything!"

"Jake, we have to try. Something may trigger her memory. His stance or his mouth or something . . ."

"Ben . . ." I spoke into a dead cell phone. He'd hung up.

Six

The Nineteenth Precinct hadn't changed much since my last visit a year ago. Civil service green and muddy clay were still the primary colors. Even the same desk sergeant. How could you forget a woman who looked like Dennis Franz and wore Lady Bird Johnson's 1960s-style bouffant?

Dennis had dropped off Aaron, Mom, and me, then continued on uptown with Gypsy Rose. She was going home to gather together the ingredients for a brisket dinner. While I'd remembered Sipowicz's look-alike, I'd totally forgotten that Clare Blake would arrive at our apartment at seven tonight. Mom and Gypsy Rose, however, were planning on wining and dining her.

When Dennis Kim kissed me good-bye, aiming for my earlobe—I wondered what Aaron Rubin thought about that action—he'd whispered in my ear that he planned to pay a call on the murdered editor's widow later this afternoon. I suspected that Dennis's motive for the visit stemmed more from curiosity than condolence.

Good! Maybe, under the guise of a sympathetic colleague, he could get some answers that the police
wouldn't.

I resented my mother being drawn deeper and deeper
into this mystery. Ben's preemptory policeman-like tone
had annoyed me. How dare he drag my mother down
here to identify a man she hadn't seen? Well, okay,
she'd seen him, but she didn't get a good look. Part of
his face had been covered and he'd been in the shadows.

Confessional booths keep you pretty much in the dark.
Makes it easier to spill your sins, I suppose. Not having
made my Easter duty in several years, I guess, technically, I've been excommunicated; however, I often go
to church with Mom.

While Aaron reassured my mother, I wondered if Ben
would ask each of the men in the lineup to speak. Mom
might recognize the killer's voice. She'd mentioned that
he'd sounded cultured. Who knows? Maybe this hit man
had not been recruited from killer central casting, but
rather from Oxford or Cambridge.

Ben had decorated the depressing mud-clay color
walls in his office with posters from the Metropolitan
Museum of Art's exhibits—mostly Matisse and Monet.
The novels, scattered among his legal folders, accordion
files, and law books, included Fitzgerald, Hemingway,
and Maugham. My favorites, too.

The Chief of Detectives had puffy circles under his
big brown eyes. The haggard look made him totally ap-
pealing. Antonio Banderas with Sam Spade's world-
weariness. My annoyance dissipated. Under other
circumstances, I would have been turned on; but what
with his father, my mother, and the specter of Father
Blake crowding the tiny room, logic, not lust, prevailed.
He boiled water in his Mr. Coffee machine and served
Mom and me tea in matching Mickey and Minnie Mouse

mugs. Aaron and Ben had to settle for Styrofoam. The familiar, comforting O'Hara family ritual seemed to calm my mother.

I couldn't believe how much the lineup viewing room that Ben led us to resembled those I've seen on *Law & Order*. My mother watches that show every Wednesday night at ten. She has a "thing"—best defined as somewhere between a crush and the hots—for both Sam Waterston and Jerry Orbach. When the show finally won an Emmy—*Law & Order* had been the Susan Lucci of night-time drama—Mom and Gypsy Rose celebrated with a mini marathon, watching six hours of their favorite *Law & Order* tapes, while drinking champagne and dining on lobster salad and Gypsy Rose's killer chocolate cake. I'd fled to Too Tall Tom's till they came to their senses.

An attractive brunette, long and lanky, sat, posture perfect, on a folding chair in the back of the room, far removed from the one-way glass window. She held a yellow legal pad in one hand and a burgundy Mont Blanc pen in the other. Ben introduced her as Sandy Ellis—Detective Ellis—and said she'd been assigned to the Blake murder. Hum . . . what had happened to his former partner, the horrid, but homely, Joe Cassidy? This woman sparkled like a Tiffany display case and dressed as if she'd been shopping in Bloomingdale's with Jane.

Ben gently inched my mother forward. We stood in front of the glass, forming our own lineup, staring into an empty room. I stood next to Mom, holding her shaking right hand. Aaron was on my right and Ben, wired for sound, to Mom's left.

"Ready, Maura?" Ben asked.

"Let's do it." Mom sounded nervous, but determined.

Ben ordered an invisible colleague on the other side of the glass, "Bring 'em in."

Five men took their assigned places, standing front and center, facing their unseen audience. Their ages ranged from thirty to fifty. Their height, from five foot, six inches, to five foot, eleven inches. All, as Mom had described the killer, were slim. And they all appeared to be Hispanic, but then so did Ben.

They turned, as Ben instructed them, showing right, then left profiles, performing on cue. I figured there were four cops and one suspect up there, but I couldn't even venture a guess as to which of the five might be our murderer.

"Well, Maura?" Ben asked.

Mom squeezed my hand. "I have no idea!"

Then Ben actually asked each of them to say two words: "Rotten bitch."

Their deliveries ran the gamut—from amusement to anger. Two shouted out. One hissed. Another snickered. And the last one spoke the words so softly that Ben had to ask him to repeat them.

However, none of their voices could be considered cultured by any standard. I figured if the killer had been educated abroad or stateside at an Ivy League college, he'd have been smart enough—faced with a possible eyewitness—to disguise his mid-Atlantic or merely upper-crust American accent.

· · · · ·

Madison Avenue rocked. Streams of tourists, conspicuously spending money in the expensive boutiques; neighborhood families, pushing prams, heading home from their Sunday outings; older couples, strolling hand-in-hand; Rollerbladers, zipping on and off the sidewalks, or zigzagging through the traffic;

weekenders, returning from the Hamptons, jumping off the Jitney, shaking sand from their sneakers as they hit the pavement.

Aaron had elected to hang out with his son, working the phones. I think he really missed his days as District Attorney. Though Ben had sent Mom and me home in a police car, gridlock at every corner had seriously delayed our journey. We didn't arrive at the co-op until six o'clock.

Brisket of beef has to be one of the most appetizing aromas I've ever smelled. It permeated the apartment with an air of anticipation, promising that an even better sensory experience would soon be at hand. An experience to tickle your taste buds. And Gypsy Rose's brisket was the best. Drop-dead, melt in your mouth delicious. Despite all the stress, I was starving.

Gypsy Rose had set a beautiful table, using Nana Foley's legacies, the blue and white Wedgwood china, an Irish linen cloth, and the Waterford glasses that my great-grandmother Anastasia Walsh had brought with her from Ireland as part of a dowry for a future fiancé. On her thirtieth birthday, fearing she'd been doomed to be an old maid, she met and married a widowed bricklayer, John Donnelley. Then Anastasia Walsh Donnelley, complaining to the day she'd died that marriage had cramped her style, had kept her Wedgwood in the cupboard, except for a few weddings and wakes. So my grandmother Loretta Donnelley Foley had inherited the china without any chips. Mom and I used it often, giving us great pleasure, but resulting in a great number of cracked cups and broken saucers.

The candles in the dining room cast a pink glow, making all of us look much better than we felt. Since Gypsy Rose had everything under control, we joined her in the kitchen for a glass of sherry.

Spreading cheddar on biscuits, Gypsy Rose said,
"You didn't recognize anyone, did you Maura?"

"Spoken as a psychic or are you reading my mind?"
My mother sipped her sherry.

"Neither." Gypsy Rose shrugged. "I just know you.
You're sharp, with a mind for minutia. When you said
you couldn't identify the killer, I damn well knew that
you wouldn't recognize him. What I can't understand is
why Ben Rubin insisted on dragging you down to the
station on what he had to know would be a futile
mission!"

I gobbled up a biscuit and reached for a second.
"Don't spoil your dinner," my mother said by rote, but
I sensed her distraction. Murder does that.

"Mom might have remembered his voice," I explained
to Gypsy Rose, "but if the killer had been in that lineup,
he disguised it."

"That's what Zelda thinks, too!" Gypsy Rose drained
the potatoes and pulled out Mom's hand masher. An
electric masher had never found its way into my
mother's cabinets. She and Gypsy Rose believed that
hand-mashing, while judiciously adding butter, not too
much milk, and leaving a few lumps, was the only way
to go. Since I'd never had mashed potatoes anywhere
that were as good as Mom's—one of the three or four
items that she actually could cook—I had to agree.

As Gypsy Rose whipped those potatoes out of shape,
she added, "Zelda has contacted Father Blake's spirit
guide."

"Who?" I asked, lacking the willpower to stop myself.

She placed tin foil over the serving dish. "St. Thomas
More! I'm channeling him in the morning!"

Seven

Clare Blake's arrival put any further talk about St. Thomas More on hold. She was a pretty woman in her early fifties. Her middle had thickened and her hair had grayed, but her unlined skin, small features, and clear hazel eyes had remained younger than her years.

It's funny how different women carry their weight. Mine is all in the butt. I can feel it spread when I sit. Mom would be slim for life—her shape not unlike that of a teenage boy. Gypsy Rose had no angles, only curves on her round frame, yet, as Mr. Kim always said, she cut a fine figure. And looked great in clothes! Clare Blake didn't. The jacket of her black polyester suit fit a tad too tight, and her stockings gathered in folds above her swollen ankles. If I were playing *What's My Line?* I'd guess Clare to be an ex-nun, now working in a dusty, remote research library. Maybe in rural Montana. Or some place where you did all your shopping by catalogue. But I'd have been wrong. Clare Blake, though never married, wrote books on relationships. Her latest was titled *Marriage Is a Sacrament*. Needless to say, I hadn't read it.

Over drinks, while Gypsy Rose kept the mashed potatoes warm in the oven and my stomach grumbled, Clare drank a Manhattan and continued to grill Mom about her brother's murder.

"Anything you can tell me, Mrs. O'Hara, anything at all, however insignificant you think it might be. You're my last link to my brother!"

My mother shook her head. "I've told you all I can remember. It's frustrating, my dear, for me, too. Your brother's death is a great loss in my life. In so many people's lives . . ."

Clare nodded and attempted a smile. "This wasn't the first time Billy had been threatened . . ."

"When? Who?" I asked. "And why?"

"Billy always believed that only God could—or should—take a life. 'Calling us home,' he'd say. 'We wait till God is ready for us to join Him.' My brother had been as adamantly anti–abortion as anti–death penalty, you know." Clare sighed, then sipped her drink. "And he believed that our time served here on earth prepared us for eternal life in God's embrace. That no man—for any reason—had the right to terminate another. Only God can call a soul home to heaven."

"Your brother made some enemies," I said.

She stared at me. "Yes, Jake. Enemies in high places. Dangerous enemies. And a mixed bag. Criminals and cops. Fellow priests and anti-Catholics. Pro-choice advocates and pro–death penalty supporters. But none more dangerous than Nick Amas. Even Billy, who could find some good in the slimiest scum, seemed to recoil from Amas. He once told me that he considered Nick to be an agent of Satan."

Odd. Father Blake hadn't seemed the type to go in

for such hyperbole. His calm approach and straight talk
had been among his best assets in his daily dealings with
death row's condemned prisoners. Then again, Nick
Amas's crimes were truly heinous.

Gypsy Rose, flushed from the heat in the kitchen and
looking lovely, stood under the dining room's arch and
announced, "Dinner is served."

I raced toward the brisket. The rest of this conversation could be tabled until dessert.

The phone rang as I savored the first bite. Dennis. I
excused myself and took my cell phone to the living
room. He'd better make this quick.

"So, hurry up, what did the widow what's-her-name
have to say?"

"I'm fine thank you, Jake, and I hope you're having
a good evening, as well."

"There's no need for sarcasm; I'm trying to eat a brisket while it's hot," I said. Then, realizing that he'd been
out playing detective to help my mother, I added, "Father Blake's sister is here. I'm trying to find out what
she knows."

"Good." Dennis sounded somewhat mollified. "Mrs.
Taylor, between big tears and bigger sips of Dewar's—I
think the cliché is a crying jag—told me her husband
had been upset about Father Blake's memoir. Seemed
edgy. Antsy. 'Literally looking over his shoulder.' That's
a direct quote. Don wouldn't discuss the book's content
with her, but he did tell her that he'd wished he never
read it. And she's certain Don's murder is connected to
Blake's missing manuscript!"

"God! Maybe Cali did order both hits! What else did
she have to say?"

"Well, she did mention that the handsome Detective
Rubin had impressed her to no end! You'd better watch

out, Jake. The not-so-merry-but-very-glamorous widow may . . ."

I felt my blood pressure rising. "You haven't changed a goddamn iota since you were twelve years old. You were a snotty, miserable, chauvinist brat then and you still are!"

He laughed. "Okay, I love you, too. I'll let you get back to your mashed potatoes."

In the dining room, Ben Rubin's charms were, once again, under discussion.

Clare, taking a slice of Gypsy Rose's homemade rye bread, was saying, "Detective Rubin is a kind man, very sympathetic, but less than cooperative. He did tell me that he'd interviewed Nick Amas at the Correction Center this morning, then wouldn't say any more."

Gypsy Rose whisked away my dinner plate. "I'll just warm this up for you, Jake."

I chopped off a hunk of the rye bread and covered it with enough butter to raise my mother's eyebrows. "Did your brother ever tell you anything specific about Amas?" Role reversal. Now I was quizzing Clare. "Something that hasn't been in the paper? That's not general knowledge?" I took a bite out of the bread, then thought about Dennis, while waiting for Clare's answer.

For a big woman, her gestures were both graceful and narrow in scope. Nibbling on a tiny morsel of bread, she swallowed, and said, "Not really." Then she frowned. "Wait! Billy did say something odd. Repeating some remark that Nick had made. I remember because it had to do with the past, and I've always worried that the past would catch up with all of us."

Now, chewing madly, I swallowed, and stared at her. What in hell could the woman be talking about?

Mom jumped in. "What did Nick Amas tell Father Blake?"

"Well, Billy slipped, it had to be a slip, since he never discussed his prison visits or the men he ministered to there. But one day last week he'd called me—God, Billy had sounded so depressed—anyway, he'd said that Nick knew someone from his past life."

"From a previous incarnation?" Gypsy Rose had returned, placing my dinner in front of me. The aroma soothed my jangling nerves.

"Good Lord, no!" Clare snickered. "From the 1960s. Though, that decade does seem like another lifetime!"

"Who?" I asked.

"When I tried to question Billy, he closed down. My brother had so many horrid secrets. I'm convinced that one of those secrets killed him." Tears welled up. She wiped her eyes with her napkin. I watched my mother stiffen, probably concerned that Clare's mascara had stained one of Nana's best linen napkins.

I swirled my potatoes in the brown gravy. "What did you mean when you said that you were worried that the past would catch up with all of you?"

She started. Then blinked her eyes, rapidly. "Nothing—that is—well, I'm not sure . . ."

"Clare, you do want to find your brother's killer, don't you?" I speared the last carrot.

"Of course I do. How can you ask that?"

My mother reached out and touched her arm. "Jake is just as good at solving problems in real life as she is in her books. And, often, it just helps to talk."

Gypsy Rose poured us all a cup of tea, then sliced the apple pie and passed around the dessert plates.

No one spoke. No one ate. Part of my mother's waiting game. Having been well trained, I played along.

Finally, Clare exhaled. A long, deep breath that seemed to have substance . . . you could almost see it hovering there in front of her. Then the words tumbled out. "This may sound crazy, but I believe that Billy's shooting may be connected to a long-ago murder in Georgetown."

Her audience remained silent.

She rushed on. "Back then, there were no women enrolled in Georgetown University's BA program, but they could attend the Foreign Service School. The Jesuits, intellectual snobs that they were, only cared about the liberal arts curriculum, preparing young gentlemen to be scholars who would go on to study law or medicine or, at the very least, enter a master's program. So, while no women needed apply for a liberal arts degree, we were a small presence in the Foreign Service School."

Clare paused to sip her coffee. Mom gave me an almost imperceptible nod. I asked, "And one of those women wound up murdered?"

"Yes. My roommate. In our sophomore year. Billy taught English lit there. My brother is—er was—ten years older. Since I'm no brain, I'm sure he'd arranged to have me accepted into the program. Then this bright, beautiful girl was brutally murdered. She'd been in his class. The killer was never caught. Some of his other students—now all powerful players in New York and Washington—were questioned. I'm sure there was a cover-up; they all swore that they could alibi each other." Clare again wiped her eyes, leaving a black streak across the napkin. "And I've always been afraid that my brother, somehow, knew about that conspiracy among best friends."

"Who are these players?" I asked.

"Andrew Fielding and his hotshot wife for starters!" Clare sounded defiant.

Mom dropped a Wedgwood cup. Fortunately, it rolled on its side and didn't break. "Fielding? You mean Randy Andy, that Florida trailer park trash who's the Chairman of the House Foreign Relations Committee?"

"None other," Clare said. "Andy and his soon-to-be-bride were in the murdered girl's lit class. The one my brother taught. They were all very close. Andy had even admitted to being with her earlier in the evening on the night that she died."

"I remember that case." Gypsy Rose dabbed at the coffee stain.

Totally amazing! Andrew Fielding, a philanthropic, philandering, popular politician, rumored to be running for president, was married to Rebecca Sharpe-Fielding, CEO of New York City's most successful investment banking firm. The tabloids took turns featuring cover stories about the odd couple's tristate marriage. The Fieldings maintained homes in Florida, New York, and D.C. There could be no doubt that the charming congressman deserved his reputation as a lady-killer. But literally?

"Wow!" I shook my head. "Who else had been questioned?"

"Well, her fiancé, Greg Ford." Clare said. "God, he'd been mad about the girl."

"Gregory Ford, the United States Attorney?!!" How wild was this!!

"One and the same. Of course, Billy had been questioned, too, and the police did speak to me. After all, I had been Karen's roommate."

"Karen?" I suddenly felt cold.

"Yes. Karen Scanlon. Did you know her story?" Clare sounded flustered. "Oh how could you? Karen died before you were born!"

Eight

"I don't believe this!" Ben barked in my ear. "I spent an hour with Clare Blake this morning. Damn the woman. She never mentioned any thirty-four-year-old murder!"

"Strange, isn't it?" I hoped he couldn't tell by listening to me how frightened I felt. "But then, Clare's an odd one. She may be exaggerating the roles that the Fieldings, Ford, Father Billy, and she had played in the case. Not to mention her conspiracy theory."

"Since I was in kindergarten in the spring of '67, I'll talk to Dad. If this story has legs, he'll remember or know someone who will. And I'm calling the D.C. Police Department as soon as we hang up."

"You might want to speak to Gypsy Rose."

Ben groaned. While he'd been beguiled by Carnegie Hill's resident psychic—as most men were—I knew he scoffed at her ESP abilities. By now he should have a more open mind. He'd certainly seen her "gift" in action too often to attribute it to mere coincidence.

"She remembers it well. From her own firsthand experience. Not from chatting with the dead," I said. "The Georgetown murder, I mean. Gypsy Rose had spent that May in Washington, attending a parapsychology conference."

"I gather that conference occurred long after her previous life's hot romance with Edgar Cayce. Go on," he said. I laughed at the resigned reluctance in his voice. The first time I'd felt like laughing since Clare Blake had confirmed my own terrifying extrasensory perception regarding Karen Scanlon's death.

"Gypsy Rose says the shooting—did I tell you that Karen Scanlon had been shot in the head—just like Father Blake?" A good thing Ben couldn't see me shudder. Clare didn't have to tell me that Karen had taken a bullet to the brain; I'd already known.

"And his editor."

"Yeah." I sighed. "Anyway, the shooting received a lot of press in D.C. Not here, I guess. Mom could barely recall the story. But the murder had front-page coverage in the *Washington Post* for days. All five of Karen's close friends had motives, but, apparently, not opportunity. Each had been one of the other's alibi. There'd been no arrest. Finally, the Washington police had concluded that the murder had been committed by an unknown assailant. They decided that it smacked of a hit man, spending his R and R on a sex and shooting spree. Father Billy and company had been completely cleared. Gypsy Rose never connected him to Mom's Father Blake. She does remember that Andrew Fielding had discussed the case briefly when questioned by reporters during his first run for congress. Other than that, the murder has remained ancient history."

"You'd think a psychic would have been endowed

with better intuition about Billy Blake!" Ben chuckled. "Now what were all these motives?"

I refused to be drawn into defending New Age concepts—which I hardly understood and didn't necessarily believe—to Ben Rubin, so I moved on to motives.

"According to Clare, Karen had been having an affair. And several of her other girlfriends testified to that. She'd had sex the night she died. And, incidentally, it hadn't looked like rape. Anyway, Karen had kept her lover's identity a secret. Her fiancé, Gregory Ford—Clare described him as a spoiled rich kid from Park Avenue—had been crying in his beer at a Georgetown pub, vowing to 'kill the bastard' if the rumors about Karen Scanlon's unfaithfulness proved true."

"Well, the Fords are Manhattan's old-guard mega-moneybags. It always impressed me that with all that dough, Greg had gone to work for the U.S. Attorney's Office."

"I have to tell you, as weird as Clare's story may be, she sounded damn convincing."

"So tell me more."

"Rebecca Sharpe-Fielding, back then just Sharpe and far removed from the attractive, well-dressed, successful investment banker that she's become, had been jealous of Karen Scanlon and strongly suspected that Andy had been sleeping with her. The landlady had testified that Andy had been a frequent visitor when Clare was out of the apartment."

"I'm seen old photographs of Ms. Sharpe-Fielding. With those Coke bottle eyeglasses and thunder thighs, some guys might have deemed her a bow wow."

"But not you? Is that right, Ben?"

"A guy with my sensitivity? Shame on you for asking, Jake."

"So if Randy Andy had been sleeping with his

friend's fiancée—while engaged himself—he, too, might have wanted Karen out of the picture. To complicate this myriad of motives, Clare still believes that her brother had been in love with Karen and thinking about leaving the priesthood, which would have broken their elderly, Irish Catholic parents' hearts. This was 1967, before the mass exodus of priests became commonplace. And, in fact, Father Blake did resign from his teaching post at the university on the morning of Karen's murder."

I walked my cell phone into the bathroom, turned on the faucet, took two Tylenols, followed by a tepid water chaser. Why can't the taps in the city of New York ever run cold?

"So Father Blake might be our murderer?" Ben was saying, when I shut off the faucet.

I caught a glimpse of myself in the mirror. Jesus, I looked like hell. I flicked off the overhead light. "Knowing Father Blake, I don't buy that!"

"Or could Clare have killed Karen to avenge her brother?"

"Seems like a stretch," I said, "but maybe her brother's resignation had acted as a catalyst, making her capable of murder."

"What about Karen Scanlon's family? You said she came from New York?"

"According to Clare, she'd lived with her widowed mother on the Lower East Side. Karen had won a scholarship to Georgetown. Bright as well as beautiful. She and her mother didn't get along; she never spoke about her. Then her mother died during Karen's freshman year. An aunt, Karen's only living relative—her late father's sister—handled the funeral arrangements. Clare couldn't recall if the aunt had been married.

"Okay, I'm going to place that call to D.C. Homicide. Is there anything else I should know?"

"You now know what I know. Clare claims that the friends hung tight, stuck by their alibis and each other, and the murderer remains a mystery."

I didn't tell Ben what Mom said to me, after Clare Blake had left and Gypsy Rose had finished her recap of the case. But her words, like Karen Scanlon, haunted me. "Sometimes, Jake"—my mother had locked her green eyes onto mine, and spoken softly—"the past and the present collide."

Nine

The bedroom door slammed shut, rousing me from yet another troubled dream. I'd been in a smoke-filled old pub. Lots of wood and brass in need of polishing. "Strangers in the Night" playing on the jukebox. Dancing in the arms of a slim, handsome man, with olive skin and sleepy eyes. Loving his touch, the way he led me round the tiny dance floor. Then, in a split second change of dream scene, we were in a dark room; my hair—not my own wash & wear, ash-blonde style, but long and dark—lay spread across a pillow. And my former dancing partner held a gun to my head.

Modesty's noisy entrance had coincided with his no doubt fatal shot. Since I wasn't dead, I got up.

"You better have a damn good reason for barging in here—" I glanced at my bedside clock—"at seven bloody o'clock!" I couldn't tell Modesty that she'd saved my life—well, my dream life, which somehow seemed to have merged with my real life—she'd never let me forget it.

I reached for my terry cloth robe, so ratty that Mom had banned it at breakfast, and shoved my damp hair off my face. Dreaming about death had worked up quite a sweat.

"Listen up!" Modesty ordered. "Your mom is making tea and toasting bagels as I speak, so we don't have much time."

"Can I brush my teeth first?"

"No!" She pulled my desk chair out and gestured to it. "Sit."

Modesty Meade, a sister ghostwriter and a loyal friend, despite her certifiable eccentricity, made too formidable an opponent to quibble with so early in the morning. I sat. A shiver shook my soul. I suspected that whatever she was about to tell me would be all bad.

Along with Too Tall Tom and Jane, Modesty and I had solved several murders. We worked well together. I considered her a sidekick, a sort of weird Dr. Watson to my Nancy Drew—to totally mix mystery genres. She annoyed the hell out of me, but I both respected and liked her. A lot. Ever since Emmie had died, Modesty filled a most important role in my life. However, as a vacillating vegetarian, with frequent dysfunctional chakra problems and a penchant for the truly bizarre, Modesty's mood swings would wear out any ghost, friendly or not. Then, to further test my patience, for the last three months, she'd been living with a recovering cat burglar, Rickie Romero. Drop-dead gorgeous, but reporting to his parole officer once a week.

Her halo of light red hair topped her heart-shaped face, its tiny features screwed up in what appeared to be pain. I couldn't even see her pale celery eyes; they'd turned into slits.

"For God's sake, what's wrong, Modesty?"

"Something Rickie just told me."

Good God! Could this melodrama have been scripted by a boyfriend problem? I prayed for patience—to tell the truth I'm a tad jealous of Modesty's hot romance and really tired of hearing about it—then asked, "Are you two okay?"

"This isn't about Rickie and me!" She twirled her rosary bead belt. Charcoal gray, matching her tunic. "It's your mother! Maura's in danger."

How could Modesty have found out that Mom had witnessed Father Blake's murder? "Christ," I said, "did some television reporter . . ."

"Jake, I don't know what you're thinking, but don't get off track here. Rickie spent the night playing poker with some of his fellow parolees. All nonviolent offenders, of course. Rickie never carried a weapon during his entire career. He only antes up with con men or forgers or crooks of that ilk. You know, white-collar crimes. Anyway, when he arrived home at four-thirty this morning, he woke me up. But I couldn't come here any earlier than seven or your mother would have been suspicious. I told her that you and I had a date for breakfast, but that you must have forgotten to mention it to her."

Now it was my turn to wonder where the hell Modesty's tale could be heading, but I kept quiet.

"One of Rickie's poker buddies, an ex-stock broker, who'd embezzled both his clients and his company, had too much vino, then told his fellow poker players that the word on the street . . ." She stopped dead.

"What? For God's sake, what's the word on the street?"

She took a deep breath. "That there's a contract out on your mother! That Maura O'Hara witnessed Father Blake's murder!"

"Oh, Christ . . ."

"So, it's true, isn't it? Your mother did see the killer?

I'd hoped that the guy had it wrong." Modesty shook her head.

Mom rapped on the door. "Breakfast is ready, girls!"

．．．．．

The bagels were fresh. No toasting required! Mom had smeared them with strawberry butter from Sarabeth's Kitchen. She'd also put a pot of coffee on for Modesty, and our kitchen smelled delicious. Funny how the scent of strong coffee turns me on, but not the taste. Mom had a big, white towel wrapped around her wet hair and her face was covered in grease. She'd interrupted her long toilette to make breakfast for Modesty and me.

My fingers shook as I poured the orange juice. But Mom chatted away as if Father Blake's murder hadn't put her own life on the line. "Gypsy Rose wants us over later. She's channeling Zelda, who has agreed to try and contact Father's guide in the world beyond. St. Thomas More must be on a mighty high plane, don't you think? Anyway, Gypsy Rose has asked Dennis to drop by. She sensed that one of the spirits has information he needs to hear!"

"What information?" I bit into my bagel, hoping it wouldn't lie like lead in my sour stomach.

Modesty rolled her eyes.

"Gypsy Rose felt it would be rude to question Zelda. And as always, she seemed to be in a hurry." Mom poured herself another cup of tea.

Modesty stirred up a tempest in her coffee cup. "Such admirable restraint. The dead must be so sensitive that Gypsy Rose didn't dare to ask Zelda whose soul was coming for dinner."

"Brunch," my mother said.

"So will Dennis be there?" I asked.

"Said he wouldn't miss it for the world beyond." My mother laughed. "Dennis doesn't think much of seances, despite his having heard the spirits in action. But, he keeps an open mind. Or, maybe he humors us because of you, Jake." My mother, the intrepid matchmaker, seemed to be rooting for Dennis Kim even though she was about to marry Ben Rubin's father.

At least it kept her mind off murder.

"You're invited, too, Modesty." My mother stood.

"What time?" Modesty asked.

"Eleven. Now, please excuse me, ladies, I have to blow-dry my hair and put on my face."

I knew Modesty and I would have at least an hour to talk. But first I called Ben Rubin. If Nick Amas, a dead man walking, could have protection, by God, so could my mother!

Ben promised a uniform outside our co-op round the clock and that the officer would follow Mom wherever she went. Then Modesty got on the phone and gave him Rickie's poker playing ex-con buddy's name and address. When she handed the phone back to me, Ben had already hung up.

I freshened her coffee. "Thanks, Modesty. And thank Rickie, too."

"As women go, your mom is okay. Not like those bitches I've ghosted for all these years."

"You don't have to live with her!"

Modesty never joked. And rarely smiled. I thought I saw a hint of one. "What are you going to do, Jake?"

"Final answer: Find the bastard who killed Father Blake and now wants to kill my mother. But I bet you knew that."

"Yeah. I did. I think we should meet with Too Tall Tom and that pain-in-the-butt Jane to plan our strategy. I'll call them now. We can all rendezvous after the seance. And when I get off the phone I want you to tell me everything."

I would have hugged her, but I didn't want to mess with her misogyny.

Ten

Mrs. McMahon waylaid us in the vestibule. Every small village across the United States has a town crier, and, I'd guess, so does every apartment building in Manhattan. Our co-op had Mrs. McMahon. Our resident busybody and the biggest snoop in all of the Carnegie Hill area.

This morning she'd dressed for the job. A floral housecoat, featuring two big begonias, stretched across her backside, floppy mules covered her feet, and Velcro rollers topped her wispy, dyed-black hair. Her daughter, Patricia Ann, worked as a Mary Kay beauty consultant and drove a pink Cadillac. Very successful. Just ask her mother.

For years, Mrs. McMahon has been advising me to give up being an anonymous ghost and to get into cosmetic sales. Presumably, using her daughter's recommended products, Mrs. M. had circled her eyes in kohl and painted her lips a deep magenta that clashed with her ruddy skin. I've always found it difficult to believe that she and Mom are the same age.

Staring at Modesty's monk-like attire, Mrs. McMahon arched her penciled brows. "Is Modesty a member of some strange cult, Jake?"

Since the foyer is really tiny and her bulk blocked the front door, we had no way to escape, short of a full retreat. I gritted my teeth.

"Yes!" Modesty snapped. "And the world will come to an end this very minute, if I can't get out that damn door!"

You can't insult Mrs. McMahon. She had a mission and wouldn't allow herself to be deterred by any threat. Modesty certainly sounded crazy enough that I would have moved, but town criers and neighborhood gossips must be made of stronger mettle. Mrs. McMahon held her ground.

"I've been to the eight o'clock mass this morning," she said.

God, I hoped not in that outfit!

"And I had a lovely chat with Father Newell. Did you know that Father Blake's funeral will be at St. Thomas More's on Thursday morning at eleven?"

"No, I didn't. Thank you for telling me." I stepped forward. Mrs. McMahon flung a fleshy arm against the door.

"Terrible tragedy, isn't it? Not that I approved of Father Blake's very vocal anti–death penalty position! Just like that pushy nun Susan Sarandon played in that godless movie. You know Hollywood's all for saving rapists and murderers! But I say nuns and priests would be better off saving souls. As God intended. Anyway, Father Newell told me that there's no wake, just a viewing from nine to ten-thirty, before the mass."

As long as we've known her, Mrs. McMahon's favorite section in the *New York Daily News* has been the obituary pages. She never missed a good wake, ever ready to ride the subway to the outer boroughs, or even board the Staten Island Ferry, if she deemed the dead to be worthy of a condolence call.

To be cheated out of a wake in her own zip code must be eating away at her ghoulish gut.

I nodded and said, "Look, we're late for an appointment."

"Things haven't been right with Holy Mother Church since Vatican II," Mrs. McMahon said, totally ignoring my last remark. "How can a nun out of habit act like a bride of Christ? All those so-called sisters running amok, inciting anarchy. Father Blake got what he . . ." She stopped short, but I couldn't let that go.

"Got what he deserved, Mrs. McMahon? Is that what you were going to say?"

She snorted. "Of course not, Jake. You've ghosted too many mysteries. Lewd ones, I suppose. Who can tell since your name's never on the cover? But your mind is in the gutter. I'm a good Christian woman . . ."

"Hey, I'm sorry, Mrs. McMahon." Why was I apologizing to this witch? Because my mother wouldn't like me to be rude to my elders?

"Well, you shouldn't be so huffy. I only wanted to tell you that one of the parishioners saw the whole thing!"

"How do you know that?" My voice cracked.

Her narrow eyes seemed to appraise me. "That's the story going around the St. Thomas More's Seniors Society. I'd say one of our good Catholic neighbors is in real jeopardy. Wouldn't you agree, Jake?"

Trying to form an answer to that, I gagged.

Mrs. McMahon's gaze left me and traveled from

Modesty's sandals to her pale red hair. "Just what religion are you, Modesty?"

"Druid. We believe in human sacrifice." She fingered her rosary bead belt and pointed the cross at Mrs. McMahon. "Move it. We're out if here. Now! Don't make me ask you again."

. . . . .

The blast of fresh air and bright sunshine almost deleted the distasteful Mrs. McMahon from my memory, but I couldn't forget what she'd said. Damn, could Father Newell be as big a blabbermouth as my nasty neighbor? I looked across 92nd Street; a cop, young and burly, exited a patrol car and took up his post, directly across the street from our co-op. Mom's bodyguard! Ben certainly had moved fast on my request. Aaron's unexpected arrival while Mom had been dressing couldn't have been a coincidence either. He'd even wrangled an invitation to the seance.

With the tree outside our house in full bloom and the tiny garden next to the stoop ablaze with red flowers, my sense of danger began to recede. I suspected that the policeman squinting up at our second-floor window had more to do with my quasi-feeling of well being than either the dogwood or the poppies. But I paused to inhale the scents of spring.

"Are you okay?" Modesty's eyes flickered from the cop on duty across the street to my face. "You shouldn't pay any attention to that old biddy-bitch."

"You're so right. And I'm fine," I lied. "But raring to get going on this murder. Where and when are we meeting?"

"I guess we'll be eating all day," Modesty said. "Gypsy Rose usually serves a brunch that could feed the

French Foreign Legion, and I told Too Tall Tom and Jane to meet us at Sarabeth's at two."

We were standing on the southeast corner of 92nd and Madison, waiting for the light to change, enroute to Gypsy Rose's townhouse/bookstore on 93rd, when Mr. Kim came flying out of his market, wiping his hands on his apron. "Jake, Modesty, wait a minute. I want to talk to you!"

We stepped back from the curb.

Dennis's dad—so proud of his successful son—has been our greengrocer and good friend since Mom and I moved to Carnegie Hill twenty-six years ago. Not to mention that he's also the premiere poet in Mom's group of lesser literary lights—now almost thirty strong—who meet once a month on Friday nights at our apartment. I'm really fond of him and often—maybe too often— wonder if someday he'll be my father-in-law.

"Here you go, girls." His smile dazzled as he handed each of us a banana. Never in all these years have I not had a banana thrust at me when being greeted by Mr. Kim. Fortunately, I like them.

"What's up?" I asked.

"Maybe nothing." He shrugged. "Or maybe not. But Dennis said I should tell you."

Once again, I waited. As Mom had taught me. "Don't rush men, Jake; they'll speak up in their own good time." Strange advice from such an intrepid chatterbox. But it always worked.

"I didn't want to upset your mother over what might turn out to be . . ."

"Nothing," I said.

"Right. But what with that killing in the confessional—well, you can't be too careful. Anyway, I'm going to tell you and Modesty; then you can decide what to do."

"What is it, Mr. Kim?" I spoke gently, knowing he was upset.

Gesturing to the cop across the street, near the rear of the Wales Hotel, he said, "See where that officer is standing?" I nodded. "Well, on and off, since late Saturday night, I've been noticing a man hanging out over there."

"Hanging out?" Modesty asked. "What do you mean by hanging out?"

"Odd. This was a well-dressed, middle-aged man, but every time I'd spot him there, he'd be doing nothing. Just hanging out, staring up at your front window, Jake. Like he was keeping an eye on your apartment."

I swallowed. Hard. But couldn't talk. Modesty asked, "How many times did you see this guy?"

"Well, Saturday night around eleven-thirty. And Sunday morning, just after you'd all left for Emmie's service. Then again, last night. Maybe ten. Ten-thirty. When a dark-haired woman left your building, the man left, too. I'd swear that he was following her."

Mr. Kim had to be talking about Clare Blake! Thank God, Aaron would be walking with Mom to the seance. "What did this man look like?"

"Slim. Nice-looking guy. Black hair. Medium height. Hispanic, I'd say. Very expensive clothes. Like those Italian suits that Dennis wears."

"Armani," I said. The conversation I'd had with Timmy Rogers at Calvary crept out from the cobwebs of my mind. Could this be the same man who'd been visiting Karen Scanlon's grave?

I thanked Mr. Kim, then called headquarters to update Ben Rubin.

Eleven

What I liked best about a Gypsy Rose seance was the festive atmosphere. No somber channeling of the dead for this psychic. No lights out. No turban or crystal ball. No holding hands. No sitting around a table—unless a Ouija board would be in play. And, most importantly, no hocus-pocus. These visits from the world beyond were so straightforward that we participants could just as well have been attending a church social where a few blithe spirits might be dropping by to liven things up.

The New Age bookstore, located on the first floor of Gypsy Rose's three-story, red brick townhouse on the corner of 93rd and Madison, had become a Carnegie Hill gathering place. And not just for those seeking self-help or spiritual literature. Famous guest speakers, ranging from religious to racy, drew large crowds. Entire families, from grannies to toddlers, dressed as ghosts or goblins, showed up at her annual Halloween party. Naturally, I felt right at home.

The bookstore's brisk business looked more like a Saturday than a Monday morning. The two part-time sorceresses/sales assistants were checking out bags filled to the brim with New Age and self-improvement books. Guides to a far, far better life, either here on earth or somewhere out there in that big universe those authors were always writing about.

Gypsy Rose's special friend, Christian Holmes, an atheist and the religion editor at *Manhattan Magazine*, was pouring coffee. No doubt moonlighting, researching the cafe's Heavenly Mocha Blend, while mooning over Gypsy Rose. I had insider knowledge that she wanted to dump him—at least for this lifetime—but that their vibes looked good for a future incarnation. I'd gathered—from eavesdropping on her and Mom's girl talk—that Louie Liebowitz, Gypsy Rose's long-dead husband, still tweaked her sneaks and pulled the strings this go round. When I'd tried to explain all this to Dennis over dinner at Elaine's last week, he'd ordered a double scotch.

Where was he anyway? Gypsy Rose had requested his presence. I didn't think he'd skip the seance. Though Dennis has remained a devout skeptic through all these channelings, his curiosity has always overcome his disdain. And I really believe that, like the rest of us, he secretly enjoyed chatting up the spirit world.

"Is Gypsy Rose upstairs?" I asked Christian.

He was serving an elegant matron a latte. "Yes. She's whipping up a soufflé and salad. Where's Maura? Gypsy Rose says a soufflé waits for no one."

"She and Aaron should be here any minute. Have you heard from Dennis?"

Christian gestured toward the stairs. "He's in the kitchen helping Gypsy Rose."

Modesty snickered, then asked, "What about you.

Christian? Will you be joining us for the soufflé and seance?"

"I wasn't invited!" Despite his seventy-something years, Christian actually pouted. "Gypsy Rose thinks the late Louie Liebowitz may show up today. And you know that man hasn't liked me for centuries!"

"Why, Christian Holmes!" I laughed. "Has Gypsy Rose convinced an old pagan like you that there really is a world beyond?"

"It's not funny, Jake. He rubbed his mostly bald pate. "What I believe doesn't seem to matter around here. Gypsy Rose would rather visit with the dead than go out on a date with me!"

Mom and Aaron's arrival saved me from having to deal with that issue.

Gripping the more-than-a-century-old oak banister, I led the way up the circular staircase. We climbed in silence. I don't know what Mom, Aaron, and Modesty had on their minds, but I couldn't get Karen Scanlon and that dark-haired, well-dressed, middle-aged man out of mine.

When we reached the third floor, Gypsy Rose popped her head out of her office. "Come in a minute, darlings! I've left Dennis in charge of the kitchen. I'm looking for my glasses. Since I can't seem to see without them, maybe Jake's and Modesty's young eyes can assist me in my search!"

As always, the lovely little room glowed. Gypsy Rose had a flair for great lighting. The late morning sun, subdued by stained glass and enhanced by a crystal chandelier, provided a soft, rather than harsh, natural light. Ledgers and papers covered the top of the mission period desk. But that was the only clutter in an immaculate room. Mom sank into one of the gray tweed love seats. She seemed weary. A moment later, Modesty retrieved

Gypsy Rose's big, round tortoiseshell glasses from under the burgundy leather desk chair, and we all trouped to the kitchen/sitting room.

Dennis paced in front of the stove. "I think it's risen." He sounded as if he were talking about Christ returning from the dead.

Gypsy Rose whisked the soufflé out of the oven and onto the table in one smooth swoop. "Brunch is served!"

With so many taboo subjects, including the possible hit out on Mom and the man who'd been staking out our house, I had little to say. All the conversation sounded somewhat stilted to me. Aaron sat stiff and silent throughout most of the brunch. Dennis seemed distracted. Modesty, after inquiring about the meal's ingredients, clammed up. Only Mom and Gypsy Rose kept up a banter, based on decades of friendship, and managed to entertain us.

The kitchen ran the length of the townhouse from south to north. The appliances were closer to the 93rd Street entrance, and the sitting area abutted Madison, halfway to 94th Street. 1,200 square feet. The red brick floor, wooden beams, a floor-to-ceiling fireplace, and the overstuffed furniture, covered in blue and white French Provincial prints, made the space seem cozy and airy at the same time. Louie Liebowitz had left Gypsy Rose comfortable; however, she'd made much more money from her bookstore/tearoom than he could have ever dreamed of, so cost had been no concern. Too Tall Tom, whose fine craftsmanship was in high demand throughout Manhattan, had outdone himself with this design.

After a compote of fruit, we left the round oak table and moved to the sitting area for the seance.

Gypsy Rose sat in an armchair and smiled at her audience. "You all know the routine. I'll go into a trance; hopefully, Zelda will show up and use me as a means to communicate with you. She's been my spirit guide for a long time; I consider her a friend. And why not? We were pals in Paris during my previous incarnation, weren't we? Feel free to ask her anything. If she comes, that is. Zelda can be flighty. But this isn't a casual channeling; she's expecting us. And I think someone there really wants to talk to Dennis."

I sank into the down couch. My mother perched on the edge of a ladder-back chair. Aaron, rigid, sat next to her. Dennis, across from me on a matching love seat, winked. I hoped he'd behave. Modesty sat primly on a chair to Gypsy Rose's right and appeared to be listening attentively.

"Okay," Gypsy Rose said. "Relax. Talk to each other. Remember, the spirits like it lively. We hope to be hearing from St. Thomas More. He's Father Blake's guide to the world beyond. What we're looking for is information—a clue—that will lead us to the murderer. But clues from the world beyond can be much more mysterious. Way out there. So once Zelda arrives, stay alert. Now I'm out of here." She closed her eyes, took a deep breath, then her head dropped to her chest.

A few seconds passed in silence. I didn't dare look at Dennis. Then Gypsy Rose's eyes flew wide open. Her right hand smoothed her wild curls. "Why, good Lord, my hair feels bushy today." The voice, young, lilting, and Southern, certainly didn't belong to Gypsy Rose.

I sat up straight. "Zelda?"

"Is that you, Jake O'Hara? I have a message from your daddy."

Even Gypsy Rose's body language had changed. Her feet tapped and one arm twirled as if she were dancing.

"What did my father say?"

"To watch out for your mother." Zelda/Gypsy Rose shook her head. "Maura is in danger."

My mother gasped. "Is Jack here?"

"No," Zelda said. "But he's watching over you, too."

If Aaron got any stiffer, he'd turn into one of those living statues you see on the streets of the French Quarter in New Orleans.

"Give Jack my love," my mother said.

Checking out her fiancé's frozen face, I wondered if there would be a wedding.

"This is Dennis Kim, Zelda. Does someone want to speak to me?" I owed Dennis big time for changing the subject.

"Yes. Do you know a Don Taylor?"

"Jesus!" I jumped in. "The editor!"

"The one who was murdered?" Modesty said.

"How does she know that?" Dennis snapped at me.

"I'll tell you later." I squirmed. "Pay attention to Zelda."

"Poor little bookworm," Zelda said. "Maxwell Perkins and Scott have carted him off to the Murphys'. Mr. Taylor's head is spinning. Wait till he drinks one of Scott's martinis! We have to make this snappy. I want to join them for lunch before all the gin is gone!"

"What did Don Taylor want to tell me?" Dennis asked.

"That the manuscript—he said you'd understand—is in a safe, hidden behind the portrait of a young and beautiful dark-haired woman."

"Did he say anything else?" Dennis paced in front of Zelda, as if he were cross-examining a witness.

"No. Please sit down, Mr. Kim," she said. "We need to move along."

"Have you reached St. Thomas More?" I tried to sound respectful, to make up for Dennis's pushy questioning.

"He's counseling Henry. Some things never change!

But I have a message from him. For you, Jake."

"What?" I was whispering. After all, how often do you receive advice from a saint? This was better than e-mail!

"St. Thomas said you need to take a trip. But he's sure you know that. Now I must skidoo."

I leapt out of my chair, yelling, "Is that all?"

"Jake, relax! You can't kill the messenger! I'm already dead!"

Twelve

I grabbed Aaron while Mom went into one of Gypsy Rose's three bathrooms to repair her eye makeup. She'd been weeping intermittently since Zelda had told all of us that Jack O'Hara was watching over her.

I didn't discuss my dead father with my future stepfather—that is if jealousy hadn't led Aaron to reconsider his wedding plans—but I did tell him about the mysterious stranger who'd been watching our apartment.

"Ben's assigning round-the-clock protection will help, but your mother can't be left alone until the cops catch the killer."

"You're right. Listen, Aaron, is that apartment you're buying in Washington empty?"

"Planning on doing a little D.C. detective work?" Aaron sounded like the tough New York District Attorney he'd been.

"Did Ben fill you in on Clare Blake's conspiracy theory?"

"Yes. Interesting. But I find it hard to believe that an

unsolved murder from thirty-four years ago could be connected to Billy Blake's death."

"You're probably right." I smiled. Almost flirting. The way my mother always dealt with men. She would have been proud of me. "I'm thinking that Mom could use a change of scenery. Getting her out of Manhattan for a day or two wouldn't hurt. Especially if no one knew where she'd gone. We'd do some sight-seeing. They've finished the Washington Monument's face-lift and then there's this great exhibition at the Smithsonian. And, yes, we might spend some time digging around in Father Blake's past, checking out the salad days of those now famous players who'd been his college friends . . . if you would come, too."

I didn't really want him with us, but I knew this pitch would never fly if he couldn't tag along. "Maybe Mom's been right from the start and Cali had nothing to do with the murder. Though, based on Mr. Kim's description, I'd say that the Armani-clad dude who staked out our apartment smacked of Mafia. Local mob, Mexican, whatever . . ."

"I'm buying the apartment from friends. He's Foreign Service, recently transferred to Rome. Their villa there came fully equipped so they left their furniture behind for my use. But it's nothing your mother would like. I figured we'd put the stuff in storage. If we do go down there, Maura could decide how she'd like to redecorate the place." He frowned. "When would you want to leave?"

"The sooner the better. Tonight?"

"Your mother and I are going to some fancy affair with the mayor tonight. How about tomorrow morning? The nine-thirty shuttle from La Guardia? And I promise you, Maura won't be alone for a moment till we board that plane."

Grateful, I kissed him on the cheek. "Thanks, Aaron."

He grinned. "That's what stepfathers are for."

My mother emerged from the bathroom all smiles. Aaron took her in his arms and said, "You have an appointment at Elizabeth Arden's Salon and I'm going with you. I have a case I need to read up on while you're becoming even more beautiful."

Mom kissed his other cheek. The "Wedding March," loud and clear, paraded through my head.

Modesty appeared, carrying a doggie bag full of goodies. We walked down the stairs, out of the bookstore, and into bright enough to be intrusive sunlight.

"I'll catch up with you later. I'm going home to see Rickie." Modesty actually blushed.

Love in the afternoon? It would have to be a quickie.

"Bringing him a little lunch?"

"Rickie loves Gypsy Rose's homemade bread. And I'm going to ask him if he can think of anyone from his prison days who might know something about Nick Amas. Something the cops don't know. Okay. See you at Sarabeth's. And don't bring any real ghosts with you, Jake."

Modesty never attempted humor, but sometimes she made me giggle.

"I would like to bring Dennis."

She scowled, hailed a cab, then apparently had a change of heart. "It's your murder. I guess we need all the help we can get. Even hotshot Dennis Kim." A cab screeched to a halt. She hopped in, then shouted out the open window—doesn't any taxi in this city have a working air conditioner?—"Do you want me to go to Washington with you?"

Was everyone a goddamn mind reader? The driver sped away before I could answer her.

"Boo!" Dennis Kim whispered, blowing into my ear.

As always, the tingle from his touch traveled to my feet, heating up all my body parts on its way down.

"Dennis, can you meet me and the ghosts at Sarabeth's at one-thirty? It's important."

"Contrary to the public's perception, entertainment attorneys do work for a living. Much as I'd love to spend some time with you guys, I have to get back to the office! And, anyway, who could eat again at one-thirty?"

I glared at him.

"Hey, I have appointments this afternoon, Jake. Clients have been cooling their heels all morning, while I've been chatting with your dead friends."

"But I have new information on Father Blake's murder! Just have a cup of coffee, I'll talk fast . . ."

"Like you don't always . . ."

"This is information that you need to know. I might even be able to clue you in on that dark-haired girl's identity."

His square jaw slackened. "Are you talking about the girl in the picture that's supposedly covering up a safe containing Billy Blake's manuscript?"

"That's the one."

The old "need to know" line had worked again. I grinned as Dennis pulled out a space-age micro-mini cell phone, almost as slim as a credit card, and started punching in numbers. Then I used my phone to call Ben. I wanted to fill him in on the seance. Dennis and I—a thoroughly modern couple—stood, back-to-back on the corner of Madison Avenue and 93rd Street, amid the midday throngs, cell phones activated, voices raised, communicating, but not with each other.

. . . . .

While Too Tall Tom wolfed down an order of French toast and a plate of pasta primavera—having so much space to fill, he always ate two entrees—and Jane nibbled on a fruit salad, Dennis, Modesty, and I drank tea. Too many cups. And, despite Gypsy Rose's great brunch not yet hitting my digestive track, I couldn't resist downing one or two of Sarabeth's biscuits, spread with strawberry butter. Jane, on a lifetime diet, wasn't eating hers anyway.

Well aware that Ben Rubin would have a fit, I'd also been spoon-feeding the ghosts and Dennis all the strange twists and turns in the case. Or rather in the two cases, now totally convinced that the Scanlon and Blake murders were linked.

Beginning at Karen Scanlon's grave site, followed by Clare Blake's startling story, finishing with Mr. Kim's tale of the mysterious stranger who'd been watching our apartment, I held everyone's complete attention. Even Dennis's and Modesty's. And they each had been aware of some of the plot points.

Too Tall Tom whistled. Impressed with my revelations or calling the waitress? I couldn't be sure. He did order the deep dish apple pie when she appeared.

Jane, however, appeared duly impressed. "Isn't Greg Ford way too handsome? And all that money. He never married, you know, maybe he's still in love with a dead woman. And the Fieldings? I've always thought they were such a fascinating couple. Such a progressive marriage. She's based in Manhattan. The chairman's in D.C. Then they holiday together in Palm Beach. And it really seems to work!"

"You're suffering from *In Style* celebrity syndrome," Modesty snarled. "Fatal, you know; first it leaves the reader brain-dead. Then the other muscles atrophy. Sad, Jane. I'd say that you must be in stage three. Not long to go!"

"Cynics die young, Modesty." Jane, one of the city's

highest paid ghosts, laughed. "Chances are I'll be giving your eulogy! Have you checked your second chakra lately?"

Jane had hit below the belt. According to Modesty, a big believer in the energetics of healing, our second chakras are the centers of control over our sexual lives and interpersonal skills. Energy leakage from this site causes miserable relationships, wicked jealousies, and serious addictions.

Too Tall Tom shoved pie aside. "You two just shut up! Stop this nasty behavior. Right this very minute! Maura is in danger and your bickering isn't going to help her or Jake!"

Dennis poured another cup of tea and snatched a biscuit from my plate.

Modesty twirled her beads and changed the subject. "Are you going down to Washington, Jake?"

"Yes. With Mom and Aaron. But, if there's a hit out on my mother, I don't want anyone to know where we've gone. That includes Rickie." I met Modesty's eyes. "Working on the Scanlon murder will keep Mom busy. We'll be back in time for Father Blake's wake and funeral mass at St. Thomas More's on Thursday morning."

"Well, much as I dislike meddling with murder and interviewing prospective killers, I'm ready to help!" Jane clapped her hands. That action and her beatific smile belied her words. "Can I have Andy Fielding? Did you know that he made *People* magazine's latest one hundred most beautiful list?"

"The Fieldings are mine!" Too Tall Tom wagged a finger at Jane. "Who says New York is a city where no one knows anyone? At Tess Youngblood's—you know, the editor at *Northern Living*—suggestion, I met with a new client this morning. Not three hours ago! To redo a huge—positively massive—twelve-room co-op on Fifth. Jackie O's old building. The building management has certainly let down their standards since her death! After a bout of negotiations that would have decimated a lesser man, I got the job!" Too Tall Tom made much more money as Manhattan's finest carpenter/decorator than as a how-to handyman ghost. "And who, you may inquire, is this bitch of a boss? Does anyone need three guesses?"

"Rebecca Sharpe-Fielding!" I dropped the jar of strawberry butter on my lap.

"None other." Too Tall Tom beamed. "We now have a spy working undercover inside a suspect's home!"

Jane, looking crushed, handed me a napkin. "Well, I don't see why I can't have Andy! He's hardly ever at their Fifth Avenue apartment."

Dennis said, "Hey, Jake, I can top Too Tall Tom. I can have you dancing in a suspect's arms tonight. Come with me to the Intra-American Trade Association's fund-raiser at the Plaza. I'm shopping Greg Ford's book proposal and he invited me to sit at his table. Greg may still be in love with the ghost of Karen Scanlon, but he'd never turn down the chance to waltz a live pretty woman around the floor!"

Thirteen

Dennis topping Too Tall Tom resulted in my topping Mom and Aaron. We were all going to the same affair. They'd be seated at the mayor's table, but Dennis and I would be seated at the table reserved for the United States Attorney for the Southern District of New York!

Greg Ford's other guests would include the beautiful, former Hollywood star turned political activist Lilly Turner, the Chairman of the House Foreign Relations Committee, the Honorable Andrew Fielding, and his wife, Rebecca Sharpe-Fielding, the CEO of New York City's largest investment banking firm. An Academy Award–winning actress and a grand slam of suspects! What more could a woman ask!

When Mom had arrived home from Elizabeth Arden's—all buffed and beautiful—Aaron entrusted her to my care. And, of course, the police guard remained entrenched across the street. Aaron said he'd be back to pick her up at seven. Great! The exact time that Dennis would be coming for me. A second chance for the odd couples to go out on a pseudo double date.

My mother found my distress amusing. "Ben Rubin better move his buns or Dennis Kim will steal you away!" She giggled. "When his father reports to him about you and Dennis . . ."

"Mom, there isn't any me and Dennis. I wanted to talk to these people; he provided the opportunity; and I took it. Not a date. At least, not a real date. Do you understand?"

"You have to do something about your hair! And your skin looks tired. Isn't this perfect timing?" She'd held up an Elizabeth Arden shopping bag . . . filled with samples. "We'll begin with the scrub! Work on those pores!" Then she pulled me toward her bedroom. "And what are you going to wear?" She flung open her closet. "That long black linen sheath with the slit and the Audrey Hepburn boat neckline—you know, the one I picked up in that thrift shop in Southampton—will be perfect. And I think you should wear Nana's pearls. They positively give a girl a glow. Especially in candlelight!"

We'd spent the rest of the afternoon playing dress up. Gypsy Rose arrived at five to do my face and hair.

By seven, I'd been transformed from a shabby *Annie Hall* into Mom and Gypsy Rose's picture of a *Pretty Woman*. Maybe the United States Attorney might want to take me for a spin!

Dennis certainly did. "You look too good to share with anyone else. Let's drive through the park. I want to talk to you." Then we fell into an awkward silence. A few minutes later, he pulled the Rolls up in front of the Tavern on the Green.

"What are you doing? We'll miss the cocktail party!"

"And, if we're lucky, maybe a couple of the speeches. Let's have a drink here."

The head waiter found us a tiny table on the patio

under a sky filled with stars and moonlight. We ordered martinis. My toes twitched. I slipped out of Gypsy Rose's sexy black sandals—one size too large and one width too narrow—but fit had nothing to do with my feet being on fire. Dennis had run his fingers along my bare shoulder and that touch had ignited my hot spot.

I leaned over—not a stretch, we were almost sitting in each other's laps—and kissed him. My bare foot climbed up his leg.

. . . . .

We missed both the cocktail party and Chairman of the Foreign Relations Committee Andrew Fielding's entire forty-minute welcome.

The Grand Ballroom at the Plaza had been transformed into a mini Latin America. The flags of many countries flew in an artificially programmed breeze behind the dais, and hundreds of balloons in those flags' colors floated from the ceiling. The band played a samba and waiters carried trays filled with rum swizzles.

Dennis and I found our seats as the soup was being served.

With the applause still thundering, Andy Fielding returned to our table, taking the empty chair directly across from me, and extending his hand. Massive, like the man.

"You must be Jake O'Hara." The congressman's blue eyes crinkled charmingly. "Well, isn't Dennis a lucky man, escorting you here tonight?" Then he turned that powerful personality on Dennis. "Nice to see you again, Counselor." Fielding grinned, looking for a brief moment like the naughty schoolboy I'd bet he'd been, as the applause finally ended. "I never can tell if they clap because they enjoyed my talk or if they're just grateful it's over!"

"Probably a little of both!" Dennis deadpanned.

I tried to kick Dennis, but couldn't make contact. No need to worry, Andy Fielding roared with laughter. I'd read that he worked a room as well as Bill Clinton ever had, and the congressman seemed equally comfortable one-on-one. With his graying, thick red hair and a face full of freckles, he looked like an overgrown Huck Finn. And he promoted that image. Country boy goes to Washington. A recurring theme in all his campaigns. A bit odd for a man who'd graduated magna cum laude from Harvard Law and then attended Oxford on a scholarship.

His wife, Rebecca Sharpe-Fielding, last year's *Time* magazine's Woman of the Year and Fulbright scholar herself, strode across the room and sat on Fielding's right. Had she missed her husband's speech, too?

Smiling, she stretched to shake my hand.

"So nice to meet you, Jake! Please call me Rebecca. I understand you're a ghostwriter. When I'm ready to tell all, I'll have Dennis give you a call. But you must promise to make my enemies look really bad!"

I laughed and had a sip of the cream of mushroom soup.

Now in her early fifties, this lady had made one hell of an image transformation from college creep to career chic. The tabloids thrived on showing her before and after pictures. Mostly from beach parties past, focusing on her thick calves and ankles. She was a native Floridian, and there seemed to be a never ending supply of the less-than-attractive teenage Rebecca frolicking in the sunshine shots.

Like most high-profile Manhattan women, she now favored black pant suits, adding a touch of color in her scarves or shawls. She'd traded her glasses for aquamarine contact lenses. And her once stringy Tootsie

Roll–color hair, held in place with a plastic headband, had morphed into a honey-gold, short, smooth style that reminded me of Mom's Diane Sawyer do.

Tonight Rebecca wore a black silk empire gown, with a sweeping skirt, falling almost to the floor, covering those Achilles' ankles, and featuring a low neckline, showing lots of white skin.

I've noticed that wealthy and successful New York women have great skin and good teeth. Well able to afford snow-white caps and fruit-of-the-month peels, they must find their dermatologists and dentists as indispensable as their hair stylists, fashion designers, personal trainers, and makeup artists. Ms. Sharpe-Fielding was no exception.

If possible, she exuded even more charm than her husband. Yet Too Tall Tom had said that she was a bitch. The old angel on the outside, but a devil at home cliché? Or could Ms. Sharpe-Fielding merely have demanded more than Too Tall Tom's talent could tolerate? That did happen on occasion. And he'd been known to hold grudges against clients who "didn't appreciate real artistry!"

Dennis asked me to tango. I remembered the night he'd taught me how. And the steamy detour we'd taken this evening. My heart pounding and my toes twitching, I held his hand as we left the table. Damn! If this wasn't love, lust might be enough. I couldn't wait to be in his arms.

But, enroute to the dance floor, we stopped and he introduced me to our host.

I had no doubt that Greg Ford would sit tall in the saddle. John Wayne. Long after *Stagecoach*, but well before *True Grit*. Circa *The Quiet Man*.

Tall and muscular, Ford had a rugged, take-charge

style, tempered with a courtly attitude. He reminded me of my father. I liked him right away.

"Jake, I've just gotten off the phone with Ben Rubin." God, I guess no one had been at the table, listening to Andy Fielding's speech! "I've offered the complete cooperation of the Justice Department in protecting your mother. Round-the-clock until this situation is under control."

"Thank you, Mr. Ford."

"Your mother is a wonderful lady." His smile seemed warm and sincere. "I met her at the cocktail party. And, of course, her fiancé, Aaron Rubin, is an old friend and former colleague of mine. I don't want you to worry, Jake; we'll catch this killer long before it's time for you to catch your mother's bridal bouquet!" He turned to Dennis. "Won't that be great fun? Now, may I steal this lovely lady away from you? I've been told that I tango like Rudolph Valentino!"

And he did.

Feeling like Pola Negri, I floated back to the table. My dinner companions were on their feet, applauding our performance. Blushing, I stammered, "He made me look good." Only too true.

The conversation during dinner sparkled. Though I'd come here prepared to dislike them, I felt as if I'd known the Fieldings and Greg Ford all my life.

When the main course, not rubbery chicken, but filet mignon and lobster, was cleared, Lilly Turner, the quintessential movie star and chair of the benefit ball, dressed in a scarlet sheath that clung to her curves like Saran Wrap, grabbed my arm. "Come, sit by me, young lady, I want to warn you about Dennis Kim!"

"Don't believe a word she says!" Dennis asked Rebecca to dance, leaving me in Lilly's clutches.

The lady downed her glass of champagne, poured

herself another, then stage whispered, "Sexy bastard, isn't he? His ex-wife, Wendy Wu, has told me how much she misses their romps in the hay. He certainly seems smitten with you. Grab him! Dennis Kim has more money than all of my former husbands combined! And clever! My dear, he just sold my memoirs for over a million!"

The band played a Motown melody, and Andrew Fielding suddenly appeared. "I think this is my dance."

Feeling like an ingrate, after all he had rescued me from Lilly Turner, I jumped up, welcoming this unexpected opportunity to question the congressman. But before I could say a word, Rebecca released Dennis and latched onto Greg, dragging him to the dance floor. Staking out our own section, we boogied like it was 1967. As the beat moved on, Rebecca did the swim. Way cool. Looking good. Me, too. I had the strange feeling that the four of us had been dancing together forever.

When the band switched to a waltz tempo, Fielding, flirting, whispered, "Stay! I love this song and I love dancing with you!"

Good! Now I could ask my questions! I didn't want Andy to know that Clare Blake had been to visit me, filling my head with suspects in Karen Scanlon's death. According to Clare, I could be waltzing with a killer. So, I decided to tap dance around that. "Father Blake's death is such a tragedy. Not just for my family, but for the entire city."

Fielding's firm hold on the small of my back stiffened. "Yes. A fine man." He whirled me faster.

"Didn't Greg Ford, Rebecca, and you attend Georgetown when Father Blake taught there?"

Fielding nodded, then missed a step.

"And all of you were good friends with that young

woman who was murdered there in '67? Karen
Scanlon?"

The band segued from "Fascination" to "The Merry
Widow Waltz."

He stumbled a second time. Then, regaining both his
footing and his Huck Finn grin, said, "Ah! That's my
wife's favorite song! I must cut in on Dennis. You don't
mind switching partners, do you, Jake?"

The irony of his wife's favorite song being "The
Merry Widow" made me giggle. The congressman was
not amused.

My mother and Aaron waltzed by just as Dennis
kissed me on the nose. I watched Rebecca grab her coral
scarf and exit the ballroom with Andy.

"Look, Dennis, they're sneaking out!"

"Maybe not. Fielding told me he's catching a plane
back to D.C. later tonight. He would have to change his
clothes."

When we returned to the table, Greg Ford was
engaged in deep conversation with a handsome, Armani-
clad, middle-aged Hispanic. The United States Attorney
stood. "Jake, Dennis, say hello to Tony Silva."

Silva looked very familiar. Too familiar. Could this
be the man Timmy Rogers had spotted at Karen
Scanlon's grave? The man Mr. Kim spotted across the
street, spying on our apartment? I moved in closer.
Jesus! Could this be an older version of the man of my
dreams? The one who'd been killing me every night?

Fourteen

"Anthony Silva is a lobbyist for the Intra-American Trade Organization." Dennis chased me across the Plaza lobby. "Why did you bolt like a scared rabbit when Greg Ford introduced you to him?"

Christ! How could I rationalize such irrational behavior? Had Mom and Aaron seen me?

"Let's go into the Oak Bar and talk, Jake." Dennis caught up, placing an arm around my shoulders, and brushing his lips against my cheek. He smelled so good—like inhaling fresh air in the mountains. "Something's very wrong. I want you to tell me what the hell is going on."

At eleven P.M., the Oak Bar didn't smell so good. Decades of smoke, booze, and expensive perfumes had left a lingering scent of jaded memories. Though thoroughly scrubbed every morning, no amount of antiseptic or ammonia would ever wash away that aroma.

From the Jazz Age to the Internet Era, the Oak Room has been a favorite watering hole for the upper classes.

And those who'd wished they were. By the shank of the evening, the dim lights hid the wood-filled saloon's scars, but nothing could cover up its smells.

We sat at a small table for two, near the bar.

"You're going to think I'm crazy."

"I know you're crazy. Stubborn and opinionated, too. And you bite. Doesn't matter, Jake. I love you just the way you are. I guess I have ever since we were kids."

My eyes filled. I stroked his hand, but said nothing.

"Look, as far as I know, Tony Silva is a respected international trade maven. Somewhat of a wheeler-dealer, I grant you. And somewhat of a man about town. Never married. Lots of lady friends. Even had a brief fling with my ex. Gaining some sympathy and support from me. Kind of fun at a dull dinner party. Not rumored to be dangerous. But do you know something I don't? What's wrong? Why did you run away from him?"

"Oh God, Dennis! He's the man who haunts my dreams. A good many of my waking hours, as well. A much younger Tony Silva, that is. And the older Tony— the way he looks tonight—matches the description of the Armani-wearing man that Timmy Rogers used to see in Calvary, visiting the Scanlon grave. And the man that your father spotted watching our apartment." I sighed. "So how nuts is this theory? I'm thinking that Greg Ford's good friend, the well-respected, *well-spoken*, international businessman, and amusing dinner companion Tony Silva, murdered both Karen Scanlon and Father Blake! And, probably, that editor, Don Taylor, too!"

Then the waiter appeared and took our orders. I opted for club soda; I had a shuttle to catch in the morning. Dennis asked for a Johnny Walker Black on the rocks. He looked like he needed a stiff drink.

"Nothing there you could take to court, Jake." Dennis chuckled. "Yet your hunches are often right. Your time line confuses me. How could you be dreaming about Tony Silva? Young or old? I'd be jealous, if I didn't know that you only met him for the first time tonight."

"You should be jealous. My dreams are sexier than *Days of Our Lives*. Till Tony turns from a hot kisser into a cold killer."

"Are you his intended victim?"

"Yes." I shook my head. "No."

"Well, which is it?"

"Damned, if I know, Dennis. That's the mystery. I start out thinking I'm me. My head is on the pillow. At least I think it's my head. And, actually, I'm thoroughly enjoying his lovemaking. Tony's a great . . ."

"Goddamn, now I really am jealous."

He sounded as if he were teasing, but I felt myself blush. How weird was this? Discussing my sex dreams with the man that I wanted to make love to me. Freud would have a field day!

"Let's remain clinical about this, Dennis. Detached. Pretend I'm a client, who came to you, looking for advice. And counsel."

"Okay. But can we skip the sex and get to the murder?"

I laughed. "Getting there is half the fun!"

"If I wanted to listen to bad puns, I'd have stayed at the table with Andy Fielding. Can you try not to be a smart aleck and just tell me?"

Chastened, I tried to explain. "Have you ever felt like you were someone else? In a dream, I mean? I start out being me, but by the time Tony pulls out the gun, the hair on the pillow is long and dark, and I've turned into another woman. Yet I feel that she's still me and I'm still her. Does that make any sense?" I could hear the desperation in my question.

"When did you start having this dream?"

I gathered Dennis had decided not to deal with my split personality dream disorder, or whatever the hell was happening to me. But his question made me think. "The first time was Sunday morning, before I stumbled onto Karen Scanlon's grave."

"And you're now convinced that the man in your dreams is a younger version of Tony Silva?"

"Yes! And, while I know that it defies any logic, I'd bet he's the one who visited Karen's grave and spied on Mom!" My voice broke. "God, if I'm right, he's killed three people."

"But Tony Silva didn't go to Georgetown with the others, did he? He wasn't among the suspects in Karen's murder."

"How can you be so sure?" My dream had become reality. I couldn't entertain any other possibility. Tony had made love to Karen. Then pulled a gun. I knew it; I felt it! "He's around the right age to have attended college in the 1960s, isn't he? Where did he go to school?"

"I'll check it out."

I leaned over and kissed his lips.

But Dennis didn't respond. Instead, he drained his scotch, then rubbed his forehead. "Damn it, you know, Jake, I think Silva could have gone to AU or George Washington University. It seems to me, I heard—or read that—somewhere."

"So he could have been in D.C. in '67!" I had no doubt.

"Looks like the ghost of Karen Scanlon has been sharing your bed. And crashing your dreams." He took my hand, tracing his index finger across my palm. "Maybe we should be consulting Gypsy Rose." I heard no irony in Dennis's suggestion.

My cell phone rang.

"Jake, it's Gypsy Rose." Speak of the psychic! "Where are you, dear?"

"In the Oak Bar, having a nightcap with Dennis. Why? What's up?"

"I must talk to you before you leave for Washington. Can you and Dennis stop by now? It's urgent!"

I glanced at my watch. Eleven-thirty. But I wouldn't be turned into a pumpkin if I didn't hit the sheets by midnight. And I'd rather be awake with Dennis than asleep with Tony, anyway. "Okay, Gypsy Rose. Dennis and I have something to tell you, too. See you soon!"

We were in the lobby when he grabbed me, pulling me to him, saying, "Enough, Jake. Enough talk, enough time. I love you and I want to marry you." Then he kissed me like I've never been kissed before. I closed my eyes, savoring the moment, thinking how much I loved him, too. When I opened them, my mother and Aaron were exiting the elevator, gaping at Dennis and me.

. . . . .

Gypsy Rose served herbal tea and sweet biscuits at her oak table. Her kitchen comforted me. She wore an ice blue satin, Carole Lombard–like, 1930s lounging outfit. A matching ribbon held back her hair. When I thought about what I wore to bed, I figured maybe I deserved Tony. Gypsy Rose probably traded quips with William Powell in her dreams.

"There's no easy way to tell you this, darling," she began, fiddling with a dolman sleeve. "I had a visit from Zelda earlier this evening."

"Is my father all right?"

Out of the corner of my eye, I saw Dennis smirk. If he wanted to marry me, he'd better get used to these conversations!

"He's fine, Jake. It's you I'm worried about." Even in the soft lighting, I could see the strain on her face. "I asked Zelda to contact Karen Scanlon. I thought maybe she could put some perspective on all this. But Zelda couldn't reach her. Karen was no where to be found in the world beyond!"

"But she's dead," I said. "She has to be there!"

"Well, I asked Zelda to check around on the different planes, and get back to me . . ."

"And?"

"After about an hour, she returned to report that Karen Scanlon has been reincarnated as . . . JAKE O'HARA! And Zelda's Master Guide says it's your destiny to solve Karen's murder."

Fifteen

The Delta Shuttle was housed in the old Marine Air Terminal on the outer reaches of La Guardia Airport in Queens. Before WW II, the glamorous trans-Atlantic Pan American Clipper Ships landed here.

In the late 1940s, Mom and Emmie's mother would hike over to La Guardia, setting up their picnic lunch between the Marine and the Main Terminals. Then they'd spend the afternoon hanging out at the gates of incoming flights from the West Coast, hoping to ogle any arriving movie stars. That's how my mother wound up with an autographed glossy of Vera Ellen—a pretty blonde who'd danced her way through some memorable MGM 1940s and 1950s musicals. Not worth much in today's celebrity souvenir market, but the photograph had thrilled the eleven-year-old Maura Foley "to death!"

The shuttle from New York to D.C. has to be one of America's greatest equalizers. With only one class—cattle, as Aaron had joked—shuttle flights offered neither seat segregation nor socioeconomic distinction.

Mom, Aaron, and I sat in the boarding area, break-
fasting on lukewarm tea and stale sticky buns, reading
Delta's free newspapers and magazines, thereby avoid-
ing conversation, surrounded by our fellow passengers,
who ranged from a well-suited senator to a scruffy teen-
ager in cutoffs. And, off in a quiet corner, Mom's all-
time favorite television star, Mary Tyler Moore, also
waited with her much younger doctor husband. I wondered why they were flying to Washington. I wondered
why we were.

After Gypsy Rose's amazing revelations, I'd made an
conscious effort to erase Karen Scanlon from my mind.
While I'd had a dream-free night—mostly because I'd
been too edgy to get much sleep—she wouldn't go
away. I'd lain awake. Tossing and thinking. Could Jake
O'Hara really be the reincarnation of Karen Scanlon?

I felt invaded by a body snatcher who was trying to
control my thoughts. I vacillated between wanting to
solve her murder and wanting to take back my life. Were
those conflicting emotions? Or were they part of the
same soul-searching goals?

Dennis had insisted on driving us to the airport. We'd
sailed up the FDR Drive—most of the traffic had been
heading downtown—crossed the Triborough Bridge in
record time, and arrived at the shuttle in a half hour.
He'd wanted to close his office for the day, but I'd
squashed that idea. Bad enough Mom and Aaron had
witnessed our love scene in the Plaza lobby, I didn't
need Dennis sprouting inappropriate dialogue and making romantic overtures under Ben's father's nose from
here to D.C. and back.

Damn, I didn't know what the hell I needed. Or
wanted. At eight A.M., before we'd left Carnegie Hill,
I'd dialed Ben's office to update him on my dinner with
the former Georgetown crew of suspects and, if the spirit

moved me, to discuss Gypsy Rose's latest channeling. In terms of "to thine own self, be true" full disclosure, what I'd really wanted was to hear the sound of his voice.

However, a girlish giggle, rather than Ben's baritone, responded to my call. "Homicide," she'd said, the laughter lingering. "Sandy Ellis speaking."

Ah! The lovely lady detective.

"This is Jake O'Hara. Is Ben Rubin there?"

"He's tied up at the moment, Jake." The giggle had deepened to a soft chuckle. "May I help you?"

"Thanks, but no, you can't." I knew I sounded snotty. "When you get him disentangled, ask him to call my cell phone."

I still hadn't heard from him.

"Jake!" Mom's sharp cry roused me from examining my conscience. Or maybe, in this case, my subconscious.

Though I'd abridged most of the romance and some of the world beyond's communications from my report to Mom on last night's activities, I hadn't fooled her for a Manhattan minute. She'd known her daughter was sexually smitten with Dennis, long before I did. And, when she'd heard that we paid a midnight visit to Gypsy Rose's, she'd sensed that the dead were taking an active part in this case.

"Look!" She pointed to the ticket counter. "Isn't that Gypsy Rose standing over there?"

I glanced up from my unread *Washington Post*. That black straw, cartwheel hat could only be part of Gypsy Rose's summer wardrobe. Waving a boarding pass, she ran toward us. "I got the last seat!"

Unlike Dennis, Gypsy Rose hadn't asked, she'd just closed up shop to come with us!

My mother and Aaron sat across the aisle and three

rows in front of me. Mom's head buried in a book. The
new Mary Higgins Clark. We'd all been absorbed in our
own thoughts this morning, but now, sitting next to
Gypsy Rose in the rear of the plane, I could no longer
escape from my feelings. Our dear old friend often
proved to be as good at gathering information from the
living as she was at channeling the dead. And I felt ready
to explore my fears.

"This is one hell of a mess." I rubbed my eyes. "It
seems that Karen Scanlon has taken over my life, and
I'm not sure I even believe in reincarnation!"

"You didn't get much sleep last night, did you, Jake?"

Jesus, you wouldn't have to be psychic to see that!
"No, but I had an unwelcome guest. I want Karen to
leave me alone! I want to be me again. Doing a solo
act!"

She sighed. "I don't think that's possible."

"What? Why would you say such a thing?!"

"Because I believe that you and Karen are one and
the same. One soul for all eternity. During this present
incarnation, that soul happens to be traveling in its current host body. Yours."

"So Karen's been infringing on my hospitality?" My
question sounded bitter. A quality I can't stand in others.
Sounding even worse, coming from me. "Just how many
bodies does this pushy soul get to inhabit, while wend-
ing its way through eternity?"

"As many as are needed to achieve the final goals of
all souls. Eternal joy . . . love . . . and . . . peace." Gypsy
Rose patted my hand. "Whose body a soul currently
dwells in is completely irrelevant. You're missing the
point here, darling. And, much as I love you, I do think
you're being deliberately obtuse. You and Karen are a
single soul, sharing the same destiny . . . to become one
with the universe. She's not an interloper, and, while it's

somewhat unusual for the present host to be so acutely aware of her most recent past life's tragedy, it's certainly not unheard of. Brian Weiss has made a career out of people revisiting their previous lives. Karen, desperately wanting her murder avenged, has simply reversed the process and popped in on a future life!"

"And, as our mutual soul's host, I'm destined— doomed, so to speak—to catch the killer and to close the case."

Gypsy Rose nodded. "I'm afraid you are, my dear. That's why I've come along to help."

. . . . .

As soon as we deplaned at National, my cell phone rang. Mom and Aaron were waiting at the baggage claim. We'd only be staying one night, but my mother had packed two large pieces of luggage, telling me, "A day, a week, a month, a woman still needs all her cosmetics, creams, and curlers!" And Gypsy Rose had scurried off to search for a porter. She'd had to check her bag, deemed too big to carry on, at the departure gate. So I took my call in relative privacy.

"Jake, it's Clare Blake. Are you in D.C. yet? I just got your message."

Clare knew that Mom and I were flying down to Washington to do a little detective work. If she hadn't been mired in Father Blake's funeral plans, she would have come with us. She'd already given me the address of the house in Georgetown where she and Karen Scanlon had shared a basement apartment and the name of their former landlady. Though I suspected that I wouldn't find any fresh clues there, I planned to check out the scene of the thirty-four-year-old crime. Actually, I felt what could be called a compulsion to go back there. Back there? What was I thinking? I'd never been there! Or had I?

"I'm glad you called! We just arrived. Listen, does the name Anthony Silva ring any bells? Did a Tony Silva go to Georgetown with you in '67? Or maybe he was attending George Washington or American University that year. Either way, could Karen have been dating him at the time of her death?"

"Silva's a big shot lobbyist, isn't he? Something to do with trade. And a pal of the Fieldings. I think he's friendly with Greg Ford, too. Right?"

"Right! But did you guys know him in college?"

"I didn't. But my brother and I weren't as close to the other four as they were to each other. Remember, I lived with Karen, and Billy taught her English lit, but Greg was her fiancé. She'd dated Andy in our freshman year; but by Valentine's Day of sophomore year, Andy and Rebecca were engaged. They all stayed friends, and the two couples did a lot of stuff together. Leaving the pudgy roommate and the doting professor out of the action. So they might have known Silva back then, but I don't think he went to Georgetown. He's not in my yearbook."

"But if they did know him, it's possible that your brother may have known him as well. Isn't it?"

Silence.

"Clare, are you still there?"

"I'm here." Her voice had lost its assurance.

"Well, what about it? Do you think that Tony Silva could have been part of your brother's past?"

"I . . . I . . . don't . . ."

"Talk to me, Clare."

"Well, as you know, Billy had this mad crush on Karen. I'd been worried he'd renounce his vocation to marry her, but she never responded to his declaration of eternal devotion. He couldn't concentrate that spring, suffering from jealousy . . ."

·"You told me that she cheated on Greg. Could your brother have been her lover?"

"One of her lovers, I guess." Clare sighed. "Karen got around."

"But she had no one named Tony listed in her little black book?"

"No . . . she had once mentioned someone—referred to him as her Latin American project—I'd forgotten all about him, figured he'd been a passing fancy."

"Think, Clare! Could that affair have been going on when she was murdered? Could that Latin American project have killed her?"

"Both of your questions could be answered with a qualified yes."

God, what a stuffed shirtwaist! "Thanks, Clare, I'll do some digging."

"Good! And I'll do some up here."

"Yeah, well be careful. I have a feeling that Tony Silva is a dangerous man. Keep your eyes and ears open!"

"Strange!"

"What?"

"Your arcane choice of language: keep your eyes and ears open. Karen used to say that all the time!"

Sixteen

The high, black, wrought iron gates, topped with well-restored nineteenth-century finials, and the tall stone columns at the entrance to the Westchester reminded me of the gates leading up to the estate in the BBC production of Evelyn Waugh's *Brideshead Revisited*.

The art deco complex's groundbreaking ceremony had occurred in 1929. The Depression, following the crash, changed the builder's original plans from six units to four. Spread over what looked like—to a New Yorker whose front door opened to reveal a few flower boxes, then yards of cement—acres of land. The English manor house theme continued, replete with magnolia trees and rosebushes rising from grass as green as Astroturf and, in the center courtyard, a huge sunken flower garden, with statues of angels and benches where the residents could sit and sun. Amazing! All this serenity smack in the middle of a bustling city.

We were greeted warmly by a doorman, who then

helped carry our bags to the front desk in the massive main lobby. I felt as if I'd been transported back to the Jazz Age. Echoes of elegance reverberated in the Westchester lobby. The black baby grand, the gracious groupings of couches and chairs, the rose-color carpet, the crystal chandeliers, the high ceilings, and arched windows evoked an era of elegance. I totally loved it. Maybe my soul—in its pre-Karen incarnation—had been a flapper!

"Decorated by Dorothy Draper, you know," Aaron said. "In the 1950s when the building went co-op."

My mother's eyes sparkled with approval.

Not having a clue who Dorothy Draper might be, I kept quiet.

"Of course it's been redone several times over the years," he explained, "but always with her style in mind."

In the 1920s and 1930s, most of the better apartment houses in Washington had been run like residential hotels, complete with all services. The Westchester was one of the few best addresses that still continued the tradition. The main lobby housed a large, well-appointed restaurant that opened up onto a lovely terrace. Several incredibly well-dressed elderly ladies, seated at separate tables, were ready for an early lunch.

Leaving our bags at the front desk, Aaron took us on a quick tour. Between the main and the center building, we found a beauty salon, barber shop, and a well-furnished lounge for the residents' use. A full gym, a great library, a small grocery, and a valet were all located on the basement level. You'd never have to leave the building!

When we picked up our bags, I mentioned that last thought to the desk clerk. With our collective promise of confidentiality, he assured us that some residents never did leave the Westchester and probably never would—until they were carried out.

As we rode the elevator to the top floor, I thought this must be where Eloise came to live, when she grew up and moved from the Plaza.

The two bedroom, two bath apartment looked out on the spacious gardens and had a mind blowing view of the National Cathedral. Much as I hated to admit it, I knew that as soon as she redecorated, Mom would be very happy here.

Gypsy Rose and I shared the guest room. Mom and Aaron moved their bags into the master bedroom. So Mom planned to sleep with her fiancé. Interesting.

We decided to have lunch in the Westchester dining room before splitting up.

I've never dined under such high ceilings. With the crown molding, the French windows facing the green lawn and blooming trees, the quiet service, and an old-fashioned menu, I felt as if I'd stepped back in time. Maybe to the 1930s, certainly, no later than 1950. The ladies who lunched at the other tables—mostly alone, some in pairs or trios—contributed to the time warp. Each gave us a polite nod; a few smiled; but none of them spoke to us.

Aaron and I ordered cheeseburgers with fries. Mom and Gypsy Rose opted for the chicken shrimp plate, prompting the latter to say, "Reminds me of Schrafft's!"

The ambiance almost made me forget about murder. Past or present.

When the waiter suggested dessert, we were ready. As Mom said, "Who could pass up the parfaits?"

I could have gone for the creme caramel, but she swayed me. She swayed all of us. Aaron had the chocolate, Gypsy Rose, the strawberry—"no whipped cream on mine, please"—and Mom and I had the butterscotch.

Served in tiny sundae glasses, much like the ones at neighborhood Woolworth counters, before Five & Tens became history. So delicious that I could have eaten three. Or four. I hadn't tasted butterscotch in over twenty-five years. My grandmother used to make butterscotch pudding when we'd all lived in Jackson Heights. I resolved to put that flavor back in my life.

We walked over to Wisconsin Avenue, where Mom and Aaron hailed a cab. They were off to see the long-retired detective who'd led the homicide investigation into Karen Scanlon's death. And Gypsy Rose and I, thinking a prayer couldn't hurt before starting our own inquiries, agreed to take a quick tour of the National Cathedral. Only a short detour, right across the avenue, its magnificent gothic architecture was just too awesome to skip.

Twenty minutes later we boarded a bus down to Georgetown, planning our visit to Karen's college apartment.

"Talk about a cold trail," Gypsy Rose said, her cartwheel hat drawing lots of attention from the other passengers. "This case is as old as you are, Jake!"

"And memories are hazy. I know. Today, Clare Blake suddenly recalled a Latin project of Karen's . . ."

"Something she'd been working on in class?"

I laughed. "No . . . someone she'd been working out with in bed! I can't help liking Clare, yet I'm not sure I believe that she *just* remembered this boyfriend of Karen's. But even more intriguing, why would Clare have been keeping this guy a secret?"

"Maybe she'd been interested in him, too."

"It's all so eerie! Last night, I felt as if I knew Greg Ford and the Fieldings. Like I wanted to go on dancing with them forever! And I really liked Greg. Nice guy.

Not bad-looking either. Even Andy and the reputedly wicked Rebecca charmed me."

She stared at me from under the brim of her hat. It extended out into the aisle. No wonder our fellow riders were fascinated. "What would you expect? They're the souls you once hung out with, aren't they? For God's sake, you were in love with—or at least engaged to— Greg Ford. Of course you found him attractive!"

I sighed, deciding to go along, however tentatively, with Gypsy Rose's reincarnation theory. And to play what if . . . the same ploy I always used when plotting other people's murder mysteries.

"But what if one of them killed me?" Jesus, I sounded like the most way out there, weird woman in the New Age movement's lunatic fringe! "I mean killed Karen. Wouldn't our soul-in-common have sensed that? I certainly wouldn't have felt friendly vibes toward her murderer, now would I?"

"Have you considered the possibility that Karen never knew who killed her? If she—well, if your soul in common—had no reason to suspect any of them, why wouldn't you like them? They were all her friends. You've been destined to like Ford, the Fieldings, and Clare Blake. Even your dream prime suspect, Tony Silva."

"But I saw him in bed with me! I mean . . . with Karen. Then I saw the gun and her bloody head on the pillow!"

"Jake, darling, you of all people should know that things—especially in our dreams—are not always what they seem!"

Seventeen

I hadn't been to Georgetown since a high school bus trip, almost twenty years ago. Much remained the same, but more had changed. Radically. The Madison Avenue–style boutiques were gone with the winds of socioeconomic change. Small stores, some quite shoddy, had taken their place. The Georgetown Park Mall on M Street provided a home for a number of upscale shops, but lacked the warmth, if not the high prices, of the boutiques that had graced Wisconsin Avenue.

A village atmosphere still prevailed. The main drag might have a different flavor, but the Federal homes located on herringbone brick sidewalks off Wisconsin, while having wildly increased in value, had lost none of their charm. Saturated with boutiques in Carnegie Hill— where a baby's imported romper could run 250 dollars— I found the mix of antique shops, national chains, and less expensive specialty stores refreshing. I didn't even object to the run-down ones.

Neighborhoods change; people change. Who'd have

ever thought that the monk-like Modesty would be in the throes of a torrid romance with an ex-cat burglar? Or that the pragmatic, brown-wren-like Jane D. would turn into a *Women's Wear Daily* fashion plate once her ghosted books started making real money? Our Ghost-writers Anonymous group considered her attitude to be more trendy than traditional these days.

I missed the practical advice that Jane used to dish out, always liberally laced with twelve-step philosophy, but I had to admit I got a real jolt out of the new Jane, too. In her designer duds, chatting constantly about color coordination or the upcoming sale at Bloomingdale's or Bergdorf's, she reminded me of Mom.

And, while Modesty remained difficult, true love—or, more likely, great sex—had made her less miserable.

Too Tall Tom hadn't changed. His easy charm, like that of the Georgetown houses, remained intact.

I wondered if my fellow ghosts had discovered any new information, then rummaged through my straw bag for my cell phone. Damn, I was carrying as much junk as Mom.

"What are you looking for, Jake?" Gypsy Rose adjusted her sunglasses. The afternoon had turned into a real scorcher.

"My phone; it's okay. I'll call when we're finished here." As I spoke, a shrill noise emanated from the recesses of my tote. I managed to retrieve my cell phone on the third ring.

"Jake O'Hara."

"I'll be loving you . . . always!" Dennis sang in his clear baritone.

"Yeah. Yeah." I laughed. "But do you have any news for me?"

"Hard-hearted Hannah," his voice dropped several octaves.

"Look, I have no time for romance. Stop singing and start talking! Do you have anything to report?" Gypsy Rose rolled her eyes at me.

"I do. Now there's a segue." He hummed "The Wedding March."

"Dennis!"

"Okay! Anthony Silva graduated from George Washington University in May 1968. He'd been a junior there at the time of Karen Scanlon's murder. And, while I couldn't find any connection to Father Blake, Greg Ford, or the Fieldings back then, he certainly has been closely connected to all of them over the last fifteen years!"

"How so?"

"Well, as you know, Andrew Fielding is the current chair of the House Foreign Relations Committee. And Tony Silva's the chief lobbyist for the Intra-America Trade Organization. The Sludge Sheet—on the Net—and those talk show hosts on ANN all claim that Fielding's in Silva's pocket. Who knows? But, they've been cozy over the last decade or so. Now Fielding plans to run for president. Rumor says Silva will be his biggest, albeit never acknowledged, campaign contributor. The real mystery here is how did Tony come by all this dough? He'd been a dirt-poor scholarship student from Central America at GW. Then, after graduation, instead of going back to the banana bushes, he'd enrolled at NYU Law School. Took an apartment on Broome. Not fancy, but where did he get that tuition and start-up money?"

"Damn, you're good! What else?"

"Silva's close to Rebecca Sharpe-Fielding, too. When Andy's in D.C. and Rebecca needs an escort, it's Tony-on-the-spot. I asked some mutual friends about their relationship."

"And?"

"Mixed reviews. Some said it's strictly friendship; some suggested that Rebecca and Tony have a business arrangement; some said they're sleeping together. All, however, agreed that the Fieldings have a mighty strange marriage."

"Or, maybe it's all three?"

"Then there's this. Greg Ford, Andy Fielding, and Tony Silva have dinner once a month at the Harvard Club. Ford, like most of his ancestors, went to law school there. As you know, Fielding did, too. Even stranger, Father Blake sometimes joined them."

"Jesus!"

"Are you with someone, Jake? I'm worried about you. Father Blake's killer could be watching you right now!"

"Gypsy Rose is here. She'd sense that. We're okay."

"Right!"

I didn't know that one, isolated word could convey so much scorn. I sighed. "Anything else?"

"I've saved the best for last. Guess who Tony Silva had cocktails with late yesterday afternoon."

"Who?" My mind was on overload.

"The grieving sister, Clare! That's who! I'll talk to you later. But don't trust any of these people, Jake!"

I pressed the off button, attempting to put Dennis's startling news on hold and return to my current assignment. "Now where is this place?"

We were walking through a great area. Cobblestone streets, old trolley tracks, rosebushes in bloom, and landmark Federal houses. Gypsy Rose checked an address. "Should be on the next block."

"Pretty fancy location for a couple of college kids," I said.

"Did either of their families have money?"

I shook my head. "From what Clare Blake told me, I gathered that her parents were working class. And

Karen's mother was a widow. According to Clare, they'd been estranged." The narrow old houses that we'd passed by must be selling for a small fortune. "Maybe rentals were cheaper here in the 1960s?"

Gypsy Rose laughed. "Darling, everything was cheaper then! But this part of Georgetown has always been pricey. Jack and Jackie Kennedy once lived around the block"—she gestured to our left—"when JFK was a senator and Caroline was a toddler."

"What was it like in D.C. in May of '67? Tell me what you remember, your impressions about the Scanlon murder. And the *Post*'s coverage. What were people speculating? What you'd thought at the time."

Gypsy Rose wiped her brow with a bunch of tissues, retrieved from the recesses of her black straw bag. "Too bloody hot here in June!" She was so perky and such a glamour girl, that I tended to forget she was well over sixty. "The late spring of '67. Lyndon Johnson was president, growing less popular by the minute." She sighed. "The war in Viet Nam, once just a nudge, was rapidly becoming a noose around his neck. 'Make love, not war' was the cry. The slogan for the antiwar movement and some said for the sexual revolution. The birth control pill had liberated dating couples. Premarital sex and marijuana were in. But Washington had always been a conservative city, especially Georgetown. The students there, looking forward to careers in Congress, the Foreign Service, or stuffy law firms, may have been wild in private, but in public, they presented a uniformly buttoned-down appearance. Having been taught—and believing—that they were meant for bigger things, they never wanted to be photographed smoking pot or even sporting too-long hair."

She stooped to remove a small pebble from her shoe. "Woodstock and Kent State were still in the future, but across the country, college kids were making noises. The air hung heavy with anticipation of upcoming civil rights marches and student protests."

"You were at AU?"

"Yes. Louie had just died. He'd started sending me telepathic messages on our old Smith Corona. What did I know about the world beyond? As an intrepid New Yorker, I'd always thought the world beyond began at the Lincoln Tunnel. But I knew those keys were typing out notes without my fingers ever touching them. So, I came down here and enrolled in a two-month parapsychology seminar. A professor from Duke taught it. That's when I learned about my previous life love affair with Edgar Cayce. And the meaning behind those telepathic messages." She laughed, sounding sixteen. "Louie's way of guiding me, preparing me to open the New Age bookstore."

I thought about the sarcasm in Dennis's voice. And about Ben's cynicism.

"You never have any doubts about your contacts in the world beyond, do you, Gypsy Rose? You're always convinced that you're speaking to the dead?"

"Too bad Dennis is such a doubting Thomas. And, of course, Ben is a cop. Aren't they all cynics?"

God! Had I—unknowingly—been guilty of thought transference?

"But darling, not only am I certain that I communicate with the spirit world, I just had a message this very minute! A forecast—of sorts—from your father."

"Really? What kind of forecast?"

"Romantic. He says you're going to marry Dennis!"

Eighteen

"Hey," I said. "There it is!" Truly scary. I couldn't spot an address, but I damn well knew the Wedgwood blue colonial was the right place.

The tiny garden could only be called spectacular. Graduated shades of pale pink to deep red rosebushes thrived in a patch of green, well-tended grass. A freshly painted, white wrought iron bench sat under a small magnolia tree. Roses and magnolias must be very Washington. An old lady, slim and straight, wearing a floppy straw hat, a big shirt, and crisp blue overalls—she must have starched them—and sneakers, was watering the lawn.

Could this be the landlady? "Mrs. Carmody?"

She turned off the hose, and took off her hat, revealing white, curly hair piled high on her head, before answering me. "Yes. I'm Mrs. Carmody." A clipped New England accent. None too friendly. "Who are you?"

Deep wrinkles, piercing brown eyes under gold-rimmed glasses. Toothpaste ad teeth. My mother always said that white teeth and good gums were the real secrets to successful aging.

Those dark eyes never left mine. "Don't I know you? You seem very . . ."

I extended my hand. "I'm Jake O'Hara, and this is Gypsy Rose Liebowitz. We'd like to talk to you about Karen Scanlon, Mrs. Carmody. It's really important. If you could just spare us a little of your time . . ."

She removed one glove, then the other, and took my hand. A firm grip. "Come in, I'm about ready to take an iced tea break. Would you like to join me?"

For such a narrow house, the inside seemed oddly spacious. These colonials made up for their lack of width by their depth, and by being three stories high. The kitchen looked out on a small backyard, practically overlapping two of the neighbors' yards.

Mrs. Carmody gestured out an open window, "That's where the Secretary of State lives. Well, her that used to be the Secretary of State. Unemployed now, isn't she? But she still lives there. Going back to teaching, I understand. At least we got rid of those damn Secret Service agents! You couldn't walk your dog on Madam Secretary's block without feeling as if someone would pull up your FBI file."

I felt the same way.

"Which one?" Gypsy Rose asked.

"The red brick. With the dark green shutters. Big, isn't it?" Mrs. Carmody poured the iced tea into tall glasses. "Take a walk around the corner when you leave here. You'll see some great houses."

Gypsy Rose smiled. "We'll do that. Fit in a little tour. I do love to check out celebrities' homes!"

Passing a plate of sliced lemon, Mrs. Carmody said, "Now what did you want to ask me? How do you even know about Karen Scanlon? The girl's been dead for more than thirty years!"

"Clare Blake, Karen's roommate, suggested that we speak to you."

"I remember her and her brother, Father Blake, very well. Murdered in the confessional, on Saturday, wasn't he? Up in New York. Terrible thing, foreign drug kingpins killing priests!"

"Well," I said, "that's one theory."

Once again, her bright eyes locked into mine. "But it's not your theory, Jake O'Hara, is it?"

Could this old gal see clear through to my soul? Whatever she was looking at, I sensed she didn't approve. Outside, when she'd said that she found me familiar, I hadn't been surprised. I'd felt the same way about her.

"Nor Clare's. As odd as it sounds, she has a hunch that Karen's murder may, somehow, be connected to Father Blake's."

Mrs. Carmody started. "You don't say. Now that's one hell of a theory!" Her hand shook as she stirred a teaspoon of sugar into her tea.

I felt an odd kinship to this woman, so I took a chance. "My mother may be in danger. I can't tell you why, but it's connected to Billy Blake's death. Anything you can tell me about Karen's murder . . ."

"Would you like to see her apartment? I've turned one of the bedrooms into an office, otherwise, it's exactly the same as when Karen and Clare lived there."

Surprised by the offer, I said, "Thank you. I'd like that very much!"

We walked, single file, down the old, wooden steps to the basement.

"There's a door on the right side of the house that leads directly into the apartment, so the girls had their privacy," our hostess explained.

"But it's not rented now?" Gypsy Rose asked, as I stepped into small foyer.

"I haven't rented it since the murder. At first, no one wanted to live here; then, as time went by, I didn't want anyone living here." Mrs. Carmody opened a tall, white door and led us into a tiny, tidy living/dining room. I could think of several antique stores in Carnegie Hill and the Village that would scoop up these original 1950s Danish modern furnishings, paying big bucks for the round, white Formica table, with walnut legs and matching chairs, their seats covered in faux white leather. And that red and black tweed sofa, with oversized, round armless ends. What a hoot! The black coffee table really tickled me. Shaped like a baby grand piano, its bizarre design narrowed dramatically, at one end, to include a section with fake white and black keys. This item would bring in a small fortune on Christopher Street!

Watching me, Mrs. Carmody chuckled. "My late husband fancied himself to be a decorator. Though, prior to this apartment, all he'd ever decorated was a bar stool in Billy Martin's." She drew her fingers along the fake keys. "Liberace was very popular in the late 1950s, you know."

The kitchenette, hidden behind a curtain, appeared rudimentary, at best.

"Karen, for all her other shortcomings, could create quite a fine meal on this little stove," Mrs. Carmody said. "Clare had trouble boiling water."

I nodded, hoping she'd keep talking.

"They were only our third set of tenants. I'd never cottoned to the idea. Mr. Carmody considered renting rooms an easy way to make money. Of course, he never did any of the work, other then collecting the rent."

"And they'd leased the place for quite a while?"

"Yes. From September of '65 to May 23, 1967. That's

when Karen was murdered." How well I knew! Mrs. Carmody perched on the edge of the armless sofa, and continued. "Clare went home during breaks and summer vacation, but Karen lived here year round. Worked as a waitress, full time in the summer, and worked for Father Blake, too. Doing typing, I think."

"So Karen was a hard-working young woman?" Funny, how I had a need to like her.

"Yes. Hard-playing, too. Lots of young men. In and out—like that revolving door in *Evita*. Especially in the summertime when Clare was gone. One of them even took to sleeping overnight, though Karen had denied that, when I'd confronted her." Mrs. Carmody stood, and rubbed the small of her back. "Arthritis, you know. I can't work in the garden like I used to. Anyway, I've kept track of that fellow's career."

"Which fellow?" I asked.

"That Randy Andy Fielding. He liked the ladies, you know." She laughed. "Mr. Carmody used to say that young Fielding hid out in our basement to get away from that Sharpe girl. Plain as Wonder bread, but a heart as hard as three-day-old Irish soda bread. Not a nice person."

"Was Karen a nice person?"

"Well, maybe she loved too freely. A product of the times. But you couldn't help liking her. Always bringing a stray cat home to nurse, then finding someone to adopt it. And, she was a good cook. Had me down for dinner and a game of checkers, around twice a month. Made great lasagna. She helped me plant those azalea bushes. I never prune one that I don't think of Karen. So yes, I'd say she was a nice person. Just kept getting mixed up with the wrong men."

"Clare said that Karen was engaged to Greg Ford. Did you know him?"

"Oh, I knew him. Anal retentive, if you ask me. I don't think he knew about Karen and Andy, but Rebecca Sharpe sure did! Threw a hissy fit here one night that Lady Bird must have heard over at the White House."

"Around the time of the murder?"

"How about the day of the murder?" She shook her head. "I told the police all about it, but the lot of them had alibis. Look, I have to get back to my watering. Come on, I'll show you the rest."

When we entered Mrs. Carmody's office, Gypsy Rose, who'd been unusually quiet, squealed in delight. "What a great little room!"

For a basement apartment, the rooms had a lot of light. High windows let the afternoon sunshine stream in. Clare Blake's old bedroom had been turned into a mini law library. Its bookcases were filled with law reviews, legal journals, and Scott Turow's novels.

"After the murder, I went back to school," Mrs. Carmody said, "became a paralegal. Mr. Carmody died in 1970. I worked at D.C. District Court for over twenty-five years. Have a nice pension. That's another reason why I never rented out the apartment again."

"Good for you!" Gypsy Rose said. "I reinvented myself late in life, too."

Picking up a heavy glass snow scene paperweight, I asked, "How about Clare? Did you like her, Mrs. Carmody?"

"Not really. A complete prude. Always preaching. Karen may have had a lot of boyfriends, but she lived and let live . . ." Tears ran down the old lady's cheeks. "Then someone killed her! And got away with it! I never had any children. Karen . . ."

I put the paperweight down. Gently. "Had Clare been jealous of Karen?"

"Certainly. Clare and all the rest. Karen turned heads;

bowled over any man she met. And she wasn't above stealing another girl's boyfriend. Most of the young women resented her. Pea green with envy. On several occasions, Rebecca's shouting matches made that clear."

"Did you know a man called Tony?" We were walking toward what had been Karen's bedroom. "An Anthony Silva? Slim, dark, handsome."

"Not by name. Not then. Silva's a big shot now, right? However, just before she died, Karen had been seeing a Latin type. Damn fine-looking specimen, I must admit. They spent hours in her room. I told the cops about him, too. They never did find him. Murder by unknown assailant, indeed. I'm telling you, Karen was killed by someone she knew. Mr. Carmody had been warming his stool at Billy Martin's; I'd gone to bingo that night. So she had the perfect opportunity to entertain one of her gentlemen callers. A friend, not a stranger, killed Karen!"

"Clare found the body . . ."

"Then came and woke me up. I'll never get over it. All the life gone out of that lovely girl . . ."

She pushed open the bedroom door. I caught a glimpse of the Peter Max poster. My dream scene. I'd know it anywhere.

A young Tony Silva, naked and beautiful, lay on top of the bed. He winked at me.

After a lifetime of never having done so, for the second time in three days, I fainted.

Nineteen

Gypsy Rose called for a taxi to bring us back to the Westchester. I'd recovered fast when I'd heard Gypsy Rose and Mrs. Carmody plotting to have an ambulance come and take me to the hospital.

I now sat on the red and black tweed sofa, with my head between my knees, holding a cold compress on my forehead. Not a pretty picture. When I'd refused to go to the hospital, Mrs. Carmody had urged me to lie down on Karen's bed. "No!" I'd shrieked, then staggered out of the room. Each of the ladies had grabbed hold of an arm, so I wouldn't fall. Peeking back over one shoulder—like Lot's wife—I'd seen an empty bed. Tony had vanished.

"I think you can sit up straight, Jake," Mrs. Carmody said. "Today's heat could make anyone feel faint; try and drink this glass of ice water."

Gypsy Rose gave me one of her I'm-psychic-and-I-know-better shrugs, but said nothing.

But both ladies looked very worried. I forced myself

to smile. "Hey, you two, cheer up! I'm going to live!" To prove I meant it, I drained the glass of water, then stood up. My legs wobbled, but I held my balance. "Okay! While we're waiting for the cab, I want to do an encore tour of Karen's room."

Gypsy Rose jumped to her feet. "Don't you dare, Jake!"

Jeez! Had she seen Tony, too?

"Come on, I'll make it quick." Before she could answer, I crossed the room and opened the bedroom door. As I stepped into the tiny space, Gypsy Rose and Mrs. Carmody hovered behind me.

I avoided looking at the bed. In such a small room, there wasn't much else to focus on. A tall, skinny chest of drawers. That Peter Max poster.

The rest of the walls were covered with Beatle memorabilia. The closet door stood ajar; several of her miniskirts still hung there. A pair of white ankle boots lay on the floor beneath them. All these years later, Mrs. Carmody hadn't gotten rid of Karen's clothes. I felt sad, knowing that no family member had claimed them. A large black and white glossy of a young Paul McCartney—a thumbtack through his bangs—was on the far wall. God, he'd been cute.

A red leather jewelry box stood on the left side of the cherrywood dresser and, on the right, a full length photograph. I picked it up and stared—fascinated—at my soul's former body!

Karen Scanlon had been a knockout. Even in those 1960s bell-bottoms and a black poor boy sweater. Long and lanky. Shoulder-length, straight dark hair framing an oval face with good cheekbones, a small straight nose, smiling full lips, and laughing Irish eyes.

I put the photograph back, then held on to the edge of the dresser, not wanting to repeat my swan dive.

Mrs. Carmody gaped at me as if she sensed something very wrong, but couldn't figure out the missing piece of the puzzle.

Who could?

Gypsy Rose said, "Let's go back upstairs, Jake." She glanced at her watch. "The taxi will be here in ten minutes."

We waited by the front window. Mrs. Carmody paced, quickly, covering the width of the narrow room. Suddenly, she stopped. "Your mother could be in danger, isn't that what you said, Jake?"

"Yes . . ."

"Well, for what it's worth, I never bought Clare Blake's alibi."

"Why? She's the one who put me on Karen's killer's trail."

Mrs. Carmody shrugged. "For sure, Clare wouldn't mind seeing either of the Fieldings or Greg Ford being dragged through the mud. Especially now that they're all so high and mighty. Payback time for how they'd ignored her. For treating her like a pest—only tolerating her because she'd been Karen's roommate."

I shook my head. "Sounds pretty flimsy to me. And why would Clare have killed Karen?"

"Actually, she had two motives. One—her brother had threatened to leave the priesthood for Karen. Might have been an idle threat, since Karen didn't seem very interested in him. But he'd been among her gentlemen callers, when Clare wasn't home. And, I'm sure his sister knew that. Two—Clare Blake had been in love with Greg Ford. I heard Karen and Clare fight about him." She took a deep breath. "The morning of the murder."

"Did you tell the police?"

"Certainly, I told them. But Clare claimed to have been visiting her brother in his residence at Georgetown at the time of the murder. No one else had spotted her on campus that night. Father Blake swore that his sister had been with him." Mrs. Carmody shoved a strand of white hair out of her eye. "Giving himself an alibi, too. No short supply of alibis that night. Rebecca and Andy had, supposedly, been playing Scrabble at Greg's. Jake, believe me, one or more of them is lying!"

A loud toot startled me. The cab had arrived.

Impulsively, I hugged Mrs. Carmody. "Thanks for being so honest! I'll be in touch."

"You watch out, Jake O'Hara." She opened the front door. "Oh—there's one more thing. The press didn't pick up on this, but Rebecca Sharpe spent her childhood summers on a ranch in Montana. Knew her way around guns. Before her lover-boy husband ran for Congress, she'd been a card-carrying member of the NRA."

· · · · ·

Back at the Westchester, Gypsy Rose, explaining that I'd experienced a psychic flashback, had turned down the bed and insisted that I rest. Mom and Aaron hadn't returned yet. Maybe they'd gone sightseeing after their chat with the retired homicide detective. Drained, I'd just closed my eyes when my cell phone rang.

"Jake, it's Ben. Sorry I couldn't get back to you sooner. I've been . . ."

"Tied up!" I said, thinking, *Could Sandy Ellis still be there*?

"Yeah, that's right," he said. Innocent or insolent? I couldn't tell. "All hell has broken loose here. Cali and company—three attorneys and a bishop from Mexico City—arrived in New York around noon. He checked his sister into Sloan-Kettering. I guess there'd been no cure at Guadeloupe. Then he walked into the Nineteenth and asked to speak to me!"

"Wow! Don't tell me he confessed!"

"To the contrary. Said he'd come in the spirit of cooperation among our two great neighboring countries. Talked about his moral duty and his devotion to God. Told me his sister is dying. Swore on the Blessed Virgin, on all the saints, on his eternal soul's salvation, on his own sister's entrance into the kingdom of heaven, that he had nothing whatsoever to do with Father Blake's tragic, cold-blooded murder. Would he, who so loved Jesus and the Madonna, order a priest killed in church? And, moreover, he had no motive. Even if Nick Amas had incriminated him while confessing to Billy Blake— not that Amas could have had any reason to have done so—Cali, as a devout Catholic—not to mention as a respected, legitimate international businessman— wouldn't have been concerned . . ."

"The seal of the confessional! Just like Mom said!"

"You got it!"

"What did you do?"

"Called Greg Ford. We'd agreed to handle this one together."

"Where is Senor Cali now?"

"Downtown at the Federal Correctional Center. It's Ford's turn to question him. But he won't be there for long. Those high-priced attorneys should have him out of there in a couple of hours."

"Isn't that where Nick Amas is being held?"

"Yes." Ben sighed. "Greg Ford has arranged for Cali and Amas to have a sit down. Face-to-face."

"But you're not so sure that's a good idea?"

"At this point, I don't know what to think. Even allowing for Cali's religious and patriotic histrionics, now I'm not so sure that he ordered the hit."

"God . . ."

"Hang on a minute!" Ben put me on hold. My mind

agog, I wondered if I'd been chasing after bad dreams and worse information.

"Jake! I'm on my way downtown. Nick Amas tried to kill himself." He hung up.

Twenty

I lay on the bed, eyes wide open, head pounding. How could Nick Amas have attempted suicide? Hadn't he been assigned extra guards? What had he used? I doubted he'd have a razor blade handy in his cell. The really important questions would be, Why? and Why now? Most executions weren't carried out for years, if at all. After decades of appeals, more and more death sentences were being overturned. DNA testing proving the condemned man or woman to be not guilty. Or the death sentence commuted to life in prison.

Of course, that nasty Nick Amas had sent those body parts to the Federal Prosecutor. Bragging. Showing off. Taunting. So, during the appeals process in his case, maybe, he wouldn't have had a leg to stand on. Yuck! Really bad gallows humor, Jake!

Could his upcoming meeting with Senor Cali, scheduled for late this afternoon, have been the catalyst that drove Amas to suicide? Could Cali, despite Ben's recent reservations and Mom's seal-of-the-confessional theory, be the man behind the hit on Father Blake?

The four o'clock heat was unrelenting. Even with the air on full blast. The walls were streaked with sun rays, bits of dust dancing in their light. Washington in June. God, what would July, August, and steamy September be like? Mom and Aaron had better invest in a bigger, more efficient air conditioner.

"Jake!" My mother burst into the room, carrying plastic bags with the giant logo sprawled across them. "Darling, are you okay? Gypsy Rose says you fainted—again!"

For God's sake! You'd think Gypsy Rose would sense when to keep her mouth shut!

"I'm fine. Just too hot in here." I propped my head up on the pillows and smiled. "Any ice cream, needing to be eaten before it melts, in those bags?"

She smiled back. "Yes!"

After washing my face and applying blush and lipstick, so my mother wouldn't rant on and on about how I looked like death warmed over, I joined her and Gypsy Rose at the dining room table. Afternoon tea. Fortunately a moveable feast. From Carnegie Hill to D.C. Served with Social Tea cookies and Edy's French vanilla. I checked my watch. Four forty-five. We'd be having a late dinner.

"Where's Aaron?" I asked.

My mother poured, then passed me a cup of Lipton's. "On the phone with the United States Attorney's office. Nick Amas tried to kill himself."

"Yes, I know. I'd been talking to Ben when he got the news." I reached for my dish of ice cream. "Though we're only camping out here, is there any chocolate syrup?"

Gypsy Rose laughed. "I think you've recovered, Jake."

"Sorry," my mother said, "you'll have to swallow it neat. Have a Social Tea."

I took five; not Nabisco's recommended serving amount, but certainly mine. "What do you make of that, Mom? Changed your mind about Cali?"

Aaron appeared in the archway. "Greg Ford's holding Cali for further questioning. Says the suicide attempt is part of his drug cartel's conspiracy to cover up Father Blake's murder. Amas is at St. Vincent's emergency room; they don't know if he'll make it!"

I put down my spoon. "What I want to know is how he pulled off a suicide attempt. Wasn't he under tight scrutiny? Maximum security?"

Aaron, literally, scratched his head. I admired his grand thatch of gray hair. "That's what's really ticking off Greg Ford. The man sounds crazed. Looks like a guard could have slipped the knife to Amas."

"A knife!" Jesus! I felt sick. "Did he stab himself?" I couldn't imagine anyone—no matter how desperate—doing that.

"Yes," Aaron said, "in the stomach. He severely damaged his liver. They can't stop the bleeding."

"Had Amas been informed that he had a face-to-face meeting with Cali coming up?"

"Smart girl, Jake!" He took the teacup my mother offered and sat down. "Maybe one of the guards had been bribed. Was on Cali's payroll. Got the knife to Nick, so he wouldn't—couldn't—finger the drug lord."

"But does that make any sense?" I frowned. "How could Cali be so sure that Amas would kill himself?"

Gypsy Rose said, "Honor among the Mexican mob? An oath or something—like the Italian omerta—taking secrets to the grave?"

Aaron shrugged. "More likely fear of reprisal. Amas has an elderly mother and a younger sister with two kids.

Toddlers. Cali could have threatened to torture them. Either burn them alive or one of his other charming methods of extinction. And, believe me, Nick Amas understands the Mexican Mafia's mentality. Cali's one cruel bastard."

Had my Tony Silva theory been blown to hell? I pushed aside my dish of ice cream. "That would indicate Father Blake's death hadn't been connected to Karen Scanlon's after all. We're down here scrounging for dead leads in a long-closed case."

Aaron said, "Don't write off our investigation yet, Jake. Ed Wilson, he's the retired D.C. Homicide detective, thinks that at least part of your theory might have some merit."

"What did he say?" God, how I loved a mystery.

"Wilson never bought into that death by unknown assailant conclusion. Since there had been no sign of a break-in and the sex had obviously been consensual, he remains convinced that Karen knew her killer. Says he hated to see the case closed. He'd kept poking around on his own for years. Till he retired."

"What about DNA? I realize that the cops didn't know about Tony Silva at the time, at least not by name, and that DNA testing wasn't done then, but what about now? Wouldn't a blood test prove he'd killed Karen?" My mind was spinning. "He had to have been Karen's mysterious Latin lover. The man that Clare and the landlady told me about. Damn, the man I've been dreaming about!" My mother's eyebrows disappeared up under her bangs. "Dennis has been asking questions up in New York. Seems that, for the past fifteen or twenty years, Silva's been mighty cozy with the Fieldings and Ford, too. He'd even been friendly with Billy Blake, for God's sake! And get this, yesterday, Tony had drinks with Clare Blake!"

"So Tony Silva's the shooter," my mother said. A simple declarative sentence. Not a question.

Shaking his head, Aaron said, "That's really broad jumping to a conclusion, Maura. Jake's hunches and dreams are far too vague to be the basis for ordering DNA testing—there's absolutely no real evidence linking Tony Silva to either Karen Scanlon's or Billy Blake's murder."

My cell phone rang before I could "broad jump" all over my future stepfather.

"Jake O'Hara."

"It's Clare . . ." She gasped, out of breath, her terror coming through loud and clear.

"What . . ."

"Tony Silva! He's . . ." I heard Clare scream, followed by a pop. Then dead silence.

Twenty-one

All hell broke loose. Determined not to faint again, I spewed out what I'd heard. Aaron called Ben and Greg Ford. As it turned out, they were together in Greg's office, interviewing Senor Cali. The FBI and the NYPD immediately joined forces, dispatching agents and homicide detectives to search for Clare. Sandy Ellis hustled over to check out the Barbizon Hotel where Clare had been staying. Ben himself was heading to Tony Silva's. When I'd pressed *69, it confirmed that my last call had been dialed from Clare's cell phone. And I gathered that the U.S. Attorney's questioning of Cali would be taking on an entirely new aspect.

Gypsy Rose excused herself and went to our bedroom to try and channel the world beyond. Her parting words to me were, "God, I hope I can reach Zelda! Why do these crises always come up at cocktail hour?"

My mother, for once speechless, poured each of us another cup of tea. Her hand shook.

As Aaron paced, cell phone in hand, still on his conference call, plotting strategy with Ben and Greg, then sharing pieces of it with us, the house phone rang. A startlingly shrill bell.

I snatched the receiver off the dining room wall. "Yes?"

"Madam, this is the desk clerk." Formal as Jeeves. "You have visitors."

"Who?" I couldn't imagine; we knew no one in the District.

"A Ms. Modesty Meade." He sounded stunned. I wondered what bizarre shroud-like garment Modesty was wearing today. "She's with another lady, a Ms. Jane Dowling and a gentleman, a Mr. Tom . . ."

"Send them up!" The ghosts had come to Washington! Like the cavalry, charging forth in those old John Wayne movies, arriving just in time to save their friend from an impending nervous breakdown!

Modesty, in her J. Peterman smock dress—when that catalogue company had gone out of business, she'd gone into mourning for a month—looked almost normal . . . well, normal for her. Jane, smashing in an apple green blazer over tan slacks, glowed with anticipation, as if she had a secret that she couldn't wait to share. And Too Tall Tom, in a T-shirt and jeans that showed off his well-toned body, seemed about ready to burst with ill-concealed excitement.

After we all exchanged kisses and hugs, my mother bustled around the kitchen, opening another package of Social Teas and refilling the kettle.

Aaron continued to talk, nodding at our visitors, then saying, "Excuse me, I'll finish this call in my bedroom."

His bedroom. The room where *my* mother would be sleeping tonight. Even in the middle of my angst over what might have happened to Clare and my delight in welcoming the ghosts, Aaron's proprietary attitude irked me. Yet I knew how ridiculous and unbecoming that feeling was—the man would be marrying my mother. They were senior citizens, not teenagers. This was the twenty-first century.

With Aaron out of sight, the ghosts all began talking at once. Each had been out detecting and each wanted to be the first to report. Mom returned from the kitchen and played Solomon. "Let Jake go first. I need to hear a rerun of what happened today, before I can believe it!"

. . . . .

Two hours later, when we were ordering drinks in the tony Georgetown restaurant that Aaron had insisted on taking us to, the ghosts still hadn't had their chance to share. No doubt my tale of an attempted suicide and a possible murder had overshadowed their tales and theories. However, my three friends, like the entire membership of our Ghostwriters Anonymous group, excelled in both of those categories.

1789, the restaurant, not the year, had considerably improved my attitude. Its old-fashioned atmosphere, lots of brass, wood, and fireplaces, combined with impeccable service in a series of small dining rooms, offered us some much needed serenity. Our party of seven had a tiny but elegant room all to ourselves. I expected to see George and Martha table-hopping at any moment.

As soon as the drinks arrived, I tried to turn the floor over to the ghosts. But Aaron was having none of it. I hadn't seen him this excited since my mother had said yes! I guess once a District Attorney, always a District Attorney. He'd already put Cali on trial; we were serving as the jury, listening to his summation!

"The man is totally corrupt. Greg Ford has asked the Treasury Department to seize his U.S. assets!"

"This is America. Is that legal?" Modesty asked Aaron.

"Sure is! Treasury's empowered to do so under the Foreign Narcotics Kingpin Designation Act. And it's about time the U.S. Attorney moved on this. The CEOs of some major New York firms could wind up with stiff fines and long jail time, if they've violated the embargo." William Jennings Bryan couldn't have spoken with more fervor!

Modesty wasn't mollified. "Even if they didn't know that Cali was a drug lord?"

"Yes. Senor Cali's been on the department's annual designated drug kingpin list for two years now. Companies can no longer claim ignorance, and those executives doing business with the Mexican cartels can get thirty years."

Jane threw her hands up. "For God's sake, Modesty, anyone who reads a paper knows he's a drug czar!"

I waited for the explosion. It didn't come. Modesty just shrugged and said, "You know I don't read, I write!" A line we'd all heard many times before.

Aaron rolled right on. "Cali bribed a guard and then arranged the hit on Clare Blake. Maybe she'd discovered something that threatened the cartel. And I'm certain that Cali's orders snuffed out the lives of Father Blake and his editor, Don Taylor. His henchman, Nick Amas, was meant to die—and probably will. But that heinous act of wanton cruelty, having the priest's sister assassinated . . ."

Too Tall Tom objected, "We're not even sure she's dead."

Aaron ignored him, his oratory coming to a compelling close. "For the sake of America's children, Cali's drug cartel must be destroyed, then he must be found guilty, and executed."

Mom and Gypsy Rose exchanged one of those meaningful looks that only close girlfriends of more than twenty-five years can give each other. A look that I knew well. One that conveyed strong feelings. If I had to put words to the music of its mime, I guess I'd call it a look of tolerant horror. Aaron had better watch his step. These two gals marched to Father Billy's anti–death penalty tune.

I lifted my martini glass. "To my friends, thanks for coming! I'm a lucky ghost! Now we want to hear what all of you did today." I turned to Too Tall Tom. "Why don't you start?"

"Well, this is really good." He grinned with the glee of a truly dedicated gossip. "Rebecca is our prime suspect!"

Modesty, Jane, and I groaned. Then Jane and I laughed. We should have seen it coming. Too Tall Tom's M.O. never changes. In the three previous murder cases we ghosts have been involved in, he'd always believed *his* assigned suspect had to be the killer. And always took great umbrage if we didn't totally agree with his deductions.

"Laugh, if you will," he said, "but this time the murderer is mine and the proof is positive!"

"And dare I assume that the proof includes motive and means, too?" Modesty sneered.

"I'm working on means." He glared at her. "Now do you want to hear this or not?"

"Of course we want to hear!" My mother shot a look in my direction that required no translation. I nodded encouragingly at Too Tall Tom.

"Well, I was measuring for the dentil molding—can you believe this woman wants pale blue walls with whisper pink trim? In the living room yet? All forty feet of it! God, a veritable monument to gauche! You can dress a frump in basic black, but you can't get her to decorate in neutrals!" He smiled at my mother. "Oh Maura, how I wish all the world was beige, like you!"

"Get on with your evidence! Your proof!" Jane pointed her stirrer at Too Tall Tom. Menacingly.

"Picture this: I'm up on a ladder in the library; those co-ops have twelve-foot-high ceilings, you know! Ms. Sharpe-Fielding has the entire eleventh floor. The same tier as Jackie O had—grand views of the park and the museum—but the building has lost its cache."

I stifled a giggle. He'd tell the tale his way or he wouldn't tell it at all. I noticed the rest of my dinner companions had also settled back down, in various stages of resignation.

"The phone rang. About ten this morning. Rebecca took it in her office, down the hall. But she didn't realize that she'd left the speaker phone on in the library! She spent the next fifteen minutes blabbing away in Spanish to someone called Tony!" Too Tall Tom took a dramatic pause. "Of course, I'm fluent in that language, having mastered it while dating that Costa Rican plastic surgeon. He left me for one of his chin lifts. An earl. Very low in the British royal chain of succession. But . . ."

"Was her caller Tony Silva?" I asked.

"Sí. Sí." Too Tall Tom smiled.

Modesty slapped the table. "What were they talking about?"

"Laundering money! Muchos pesos! I gather that Ms. Sharpe-Fielding's financial firm is one of those New York businesses that Aaron said had better watch out!"

"Wow! Good work," my mother said.

"Congratulations!" Jane actually clapped. And Modesty joined her.

Gypsy Rose gasped. "To think that woman's husband

chairs the House Foreign Relations Committee!"

"Jesus!" I said, drawing another frown of disapproval from my mother. "Maybe Rebecca was afraid that Nick Amas had mentioned her involvement with Cali's cartel during his last confession. Maybe she did arrange the hit on Father Blake. Or, maybe she killed him herself. Mrs. Carmody told me that Rebecca's from Montana and really good with a gun." I turned to Mom. "Could the gunman have been a gal?"

"No!" She laughed. "I didn't have my glasses on, but I can still tell a man from a woman, Jake!" I wasn't so sure. She'd been complaining about needing new glasses for months.

Too Tall Tom said, "I'll bet she hired a hit man to shoot Father Blake in the confessional. Symmetry. She's hot on that."

"What the hell are you babbling about?" Modesty asked. Her appreciation for his detective work was apparently short-lived.

"Simple logic!" Too Tall Tom said. "Try to follow me, here. Amas confesses to Blake. Blake's blown away in a confessional. Symmetry! Rebecca keeps harping about it while I'm trying to build her oak bookcases. She wants me to line them in mirrors! That tacky woman is totally devoid of taste!"

The waiter, a real honey, arrived with our crab cake appetizers.

I lifted my fork. Modesty jumped up. "Come to the ladies room with me, Jake! Right now!"

"Can't we wait till we're between courses? Till after we've eaten the crab cakes?"

"No." She started walking. Then she glanced over her shoulder at me. "I have a message from Rickie. For your ears only."

Twenty-two

"So, what's so damn important that I'm missing the crab cakes?"

The ladies room would have rated an "A" from Mom the maven. Maybe not up to the Waldorf's, but as good as the Algonquin's.

We stood in front of an antique mirror, staring at our reflections. Modesty looked a hell of a lot better than I did. Her dark green, floor-length smock made her eyes sparkle. This god-awful humidity had turned her hair into a halo of soft ringlets. Mine had become frenzied frizz. And it felt like Brillo. My usual finger comb wouldn't tame this mess. I pulled out my bronze lipstick and used it as blush; spreading it up and out on my pale cheeks. Nary a word from Mom about how ghastly I looked. A direct correlation to how upset she must be!

"Are you going to talk to me or are we hanging out in here through the beef Wellington, too?"

Modesty splashed cold water on her face, then ran her

wrists under the faucet, carefully, not getting her sleeves wet. "Do you have any Tylenol, Jake?"

I handed them to her, together with a paper cup from a quaint dispenser. "That must be some headache. You never take any medicine."

"My head hasn't stopped pounding since Rickie updated me on your mother's probable hit man."

I dropped my still opened lipstick tube in the sink; it rolled, staining the porcelain with waxy burnt sienna streaks. Could Modesty hear my heart thump? It sounded like a bass drum to me. "Tell me." My voice was hoarse.

"The source is a guy who's locked up in the federal prison downtown. You know, where Nick Amas is—er—was before he tried to kill himself."

I nodded.

"Anyway, he's the con who told Rickie's poker playing pal, the ex-con, about the rumor in the first place."

"Go on."

"It's the Mexican mob, Jake. That's why I was cross-questioning Aaron and Too Tall Tom. I think the latter's on the right range, but standing by the wrong shooter. It's Tony, not Rebecca. Rickie told me that the hit man, supposedly the James Bond of hired guns, takes his orders from a big international cartel. Isn't Silva the head honcho of that International Trade group? I'll bet it's a front for the Mexican drug lords!"

"Yes. And I have no doubt that Tony just shot Clare Blake." Suddenly, racked with sobs, I staggered, trying not to lose my balance, steadying myself against the sink. But I started to slide to the floor.

Modesty placed put both her arms around my waist and pulled me up. "I promise you, we won't wait for the Feds or the cops! You can count on the ghosts to prove he's the killer, Jake. A bloody multiple murderer! Tony Silva whacked Father Blake and that editor, what's-his-name. And, I'm sure that all those years ago, he shot Karen Scanlon, too! Don't worry, we'll get him before he can get to your mother!"

．． ． ． ．

We made it back to the table in time for the main course, but when the Wellington arrived, I'd lost my appetite.

While I played with the food, cutting into the meat, moving it around the plate, then hiding it under the mashed potatoes, my head was playing mind games, trying to tie up loose ends. Too damn many of them in these murders. I decided to start with the oldest murder and make a mental list—kind of using gray matter in lieu of a yellow pad—of my unanswered questions.

Karen Scanlon's grave went to the top of the list. Why had she been buried in Calvary? Her mother had died, but what about her aunt? Her Scanlon ancestors had to have been long-time New Yorkers. Why else would they have bought a plot in Queens? Had the aunt been living in New York at the time of Karen's murder? If so, why hadn't the murder received more coverage in the local papers? Mom hardly remembered it. Wouldn't the brutal murder of a beautiful co-ed—whose only living relative was burying her in the family grave in Calvary cemetery—have created heaven-sent headlines for the *Post* and the *Daily News?* They could have fed off that for weeks! Could her aunt still be living in Manhattan or Queens today? What had she known about her niece's personal life? How could I find her? I'd brought my laptop with me. I'd do a search on InfoSpace as soon as we returned to the Westchester.

"Jake," my mother said, "you're not eating and you're

not talking, so you must be worrying. Sometimes it helps if we share what we're thinking."

Like I could tell her: *Hey, Mom, you're on a hit list. It's making me edgy!*

"Leave the girl alone," Aaron said. "She's had a rough day."

I smiled at him, grateful for the rationale. Better than I could have come up with in my addled state of mind.

Gypsy Rose, sitting between Too Tall Tom and Jane, sliced a small piece of the sourdough loaf, placing it on her bread plate and having Jane pass it to me. "Try a bite of that, Jake."

Bless her. Knowing my favorite foods, she figured that my tormented soul and queasy stomach might tolerate starch. And she was right. I ate the bread, washing it down with water, the irony of my dining on cliché prison fare in this extremely expensive restaurant being duly noted.

Modesty, sitting on my left, whispered, "What about that manuscript?"

"What manuscript?"

"Father Blake's. You know, the one that vanished along with his editor. Remember, at the seance, Gypsy Rose—er, that is Zelda—told us that the manuscript is hidden somewhere behind the picture of a beautiful woman with dark hair. I'll bet that's a photo of Karen Scanlon, covering up a safe, in Tony Silva's apartment! If we can retrieve the manuscript, we have the proof that Tony killed the editor." I saw my mother straining to hear. Modesty must have spotted her, too. She dropped her voice down so low that I could barely understand her. "I'm going to ask Rickie to pay Silva an unexpected visit. He's retired, of course, but I think this calls for the cat burglar to make an encore performance!"

Without having to give it any consideration

whatsoever, I knew that I would aid and abet a breaking and entering.

It astounded me how much stock a snide soul like Modesty had put into Gypsy Rose's seance. As I recalled, it had been Don Taylor's spirit—Father Blake's murdered editor—relaying that message to Zelda.

No question Gypsy Rose has a sixth sense, but do the spirits that she channels really show up? Or is that how her gift manifests itself? Is she truly talking to dead people or is that the way her psychic ability functions? She believes she sees ghosts, but could those spirits only be in her mind? In reality, does she perceive these supernatural truths and then credit her imaginary friends? That's what Dennis thinks happens. Or could the spirits from the world beyond actually be present? Carrying messages to the medium?

"Jake, darling," my mother said, "Jane is talking to you. Are you sure you're okay?"

"Sorry! Drifted off there for a moment." I smiled reassuringly at Mom, then gave my full attention to Jane.

"I haven't had a chance to tell you about my day." You could hear the pout in her voice.

"God, Jane, go ahead. I guess we were all too busy eating!"

She stared at my full plate, but made no comment. None necessary. "Well, my reportage may not be as colorful as yours or Too Tall Tom's, but I caught Andy Fielding in a lie."

As intended, all heads turned her way.

"How?" Aaron asked.

"Well, I phoned his office at the House of Representatives, introducing myself as a freelance writer who wanted to do a piece on him." That ploy had worked well for Jane in the past. "Anyway, his chief of staff told me that Andy would be in meetings at the

House all day, that he'd flown down to D.C. late last night, because he had this major legislation pending— trying to pass yet another bill to make our country better—she actually said that—and he'd be tied up in committee meetings all day. But she agreed to giving me a phone interview with him tomorrow at one."

"Yeah, that's right," I said, "Fielding left the ball last night to fly down here."

"Except he didn't stay all day!" Jane held us rapt. "Just before leaving for the shuttle, I stopped at this darling boutique on Lexington. In the sixties. Bought a great little bag. And when I left the shop, I saw Andy Fielding, in dark glasses and a baseball cap, hop out of a cab."

"Are you sure? Maybe it was someone who looked like him?"

"You insult me, Jake. I'm a reporter, sure of my facts!" She looked smug enough to convince me. "I followed him."

"Where did he go?"

"Just across the street. Into the Barbizon Hotel."

Twenty-three

Jane would never have waited to go last if she'd known what a wild reaction her report would generate. None of the ghosts had been aware that Clare Blake was staying at the Barbizon.

"Christ!" Aaron said, banging the table with his fist, sending his water glass flying, shattering into pieces as it hit the floor.

"Clare's hotel!" Gypsy Rose said. "Hold on! Zelda's trying to get through; she just returned from the Murphys'!"

"Andrew Fielding must have visited Clare a couple of hours before I heard that shot!" My heart pounded like a bongo beat. "Jesus, could she have been talking about Tony? Not to Tony? Did Andy . . ."

"Call Ben, right away!" My mother said.

Modesty shoved her vegetarian plate away. "So the Honorable Andrew Fielding paid a call on his old friend Clare Blake! She has too much mileage—not to mention baggage—for him, doesn't she? Where do you suppose he is now?"

"God knows!" I pressed number 2—Ben's direct line—but nothing happened. My cell phone seemed to have died. "Strange." I tried Ben's two other numbers. Nothing. He'd programmed the phone for me. Most of its bells and whistles I just took for granted, how they worked remained a total mystery. I shook it. "What's wrong with this thing?"

Laughing, Too Tall Tom reached over and removed it from my hand. "Don't abuse the phone! Those babies can be sensitive. How long has it been since you used this?"

Memories of that last gasp and final pop filled my head. "When Clare called. I think the killer must have disconnected us."

Too Tall Tom messed around with some buttons. "I guess he didn't want to talk to you!" He handed the phone back to me. "It should be okay now."

I tried Ben again. No answer on any of his lines.

"Zelda's on her way," Gypsy Rose said.

"Are you absolutely sure that you heard a shot?" Too Tall Tom asked, then frowned. "This brand phone sometimes dies with a bang."

"Of course I heard a shot! Don't I know . . ." I shut up, realizing I didn't know anything. Not for one hundred percent certain.

Jane giggled. "Gee, Jake, maybe Clare Blake ran off with Tony Silva. Wouldn't they be the odd couple?" She giggled again. "Well no odder than Modesty and Rickie Romero."

Jumping up from her chair, Modesty started toward Jane, waving her hand wildly, spilling Jane's red wine all over her smart apple green blazer.

Jane burst into tears. "Modesty Meade, you eccentric egotist, you did that on purpose!"

Then Gypsy Rose, with eyes closed and chin dropped, a sure sign that she was not herself, said, "I do believe y'all should be on guard." Zelda! "Father Blake is very concerned . . . watch out for Maura. Tony Silva . . ." Her voice faded.

"Zelda!" I screamed.

"She's gone," Gypsy Rose said.

Aaron asked for the check.

. . . . .

Twenty minutes later, we were back at the Westchester. On our way in, Aaron had managed to reserve three guest studios—another of the building's amenities—for the ghosts. Under normal circumstances, Modesty and Jane could have shared a room, but they weren't speaking. Springing for three rooms! My future stepfather just kept racking up those brownie points.

When Zelda had left 1789 as suddenly as she'd arrived, without even a good-bye, Gypsy Rose had explained that Zelda had a previous engagement with Gertrude Stein and Josephine Baker. Under other circumstances, I would have liked to join them. There you go! I'd finally become as weird as Gypsy Rose!

Mom gathered together toiletries and T-shirts and sweat pants for Jane and Modesty to sleep in. Since she always traveled with a third of her closet, that wasn't any problem. Aaron came up with an oversized shirt for Too Tall Tom. Its arms reached his elbows. Too Tall Tom grinned. "What the hell? Three-quarter sleeves make a fashion statement!"

He and Jane would be leaving on the seven A.M. shuttle. She had her current client at ten, a woman *writing* an "I Am a Witch" *autobiography* that Jane was ghosting, and then that phone interview scheduled with Andrew Fielding at one P.M. Had the Chairman flown back to D.C.? Or would his chief of staff say that Fielding was now in New York? And Too Tall Tom would be putting in another day at Rebecca's.

Probably to avoid flying home with Jane, Modesty had decided to hang out with us tomorrow. Rather, with Mom. They were going to the Korean War Veterans Memorial. Fresh out of Regis High School, my father had enlisted in the Marines and served in Korea. As it turned out, so had Modesty's. I wondered if they'd known each other.

"Maybe we can all meet for lunch before we leave," my mother said. "I made reservations for us on the three o'clock shuttle."

Gypsy Rose, coming out of the bedroom, shook her head. "I've just wrangled a lunch date with Congressman Holstein."

"He represents Carnegie Hill, doesn't he?" Aaron looked impressed.

"Yes!" Gypsy Rose smiled. "And though he's a member of the opposition party, he has served on several committees with Andrew Fielding. Should be an interesting lunch, don't you think?"

I asked, "How did you pull that off?"

"Barry Holstein's a bit of a New Age buff. Hangs around the bookstore when he's in the neighborhood. He and his wife live up the block from you, Jake. On the corner of Ninety-second and Park. Your mother knows them. When congress is in session, sometimes, Sally Holstein will come to signings on her own. He seems like a good guy, and I think he'll be candid with me."

"Good work, Gypsy Rose!" my mother said. "Didn't you and Christian go on a double date with the Holsteins?"

"Oh God, yes! To the Four Seasons. A night to remember. Sally got so smashed on cosmopolitans that she fell—or maybe jumped—into the pool! At two hundred plus pounds, she was more difficult to rescue than a beached whale!"

My mother laughed. "I'll bet Barry Holstein can confirm that Andy Fielding didn't spend all afternoon in Washington!"

Aaron and I had our own plans. At my request and to my delight, he'd arranged for me to meet with the retired homicide detective from the Scanlon case.

Mom proved flexible. "Well, Modesty and I will have lunch at the Smithsonian, after we sneak a peek at Van Gogh's White Roses. Then let's all meet at the shuttle. Around two."

Ben called at midnight. I told him how Andy had visited Clare's hotel. And how his aide had lied. And about Rebecca's conversation in Spanish with Tony Silva and their apparent money laundering scheme. I even filled him in on Too Tall Tom's concerns about the "shot" I'd heard. However, I edited my possible aiding and abetting of a break-in at Tony's.

Neither Homicide or the FBI had any clues as to the whereabouts of Clare Blake or Tony Silva. They'd tried to get a search warrant for Tony's apartment, but the judge had ruled insufficient grounds. He, too, had questioned what I'd heard on the phone. Boy, had I just moved one step closer to that caper with Rickie Romero.

"Listen to me, Ben! Clare Blake wouldn't disappear two days before her brother's funeral! Not willingly! So where is she?"

"I don't know. Greg Ford's still convinced Cali's behind all this. Hey, it's been a long day, try to get some sleep."

"What about Nick Amas? Will he pull through?"

"Doesn't look good. Take care of yourself. And watch out for your mother." The exact same advice Zelda had given! "My guy's off the case. It's only the FBI watching over her now." Obviously, Ben would have preferred one of his detectives to still be on the job. But the FBI seemed to be doing a good job; Mom hadn't spotted anyone. Neither had I. Ben sighed, "Okay, Jake, call me when you arrive back in Carnegie Hill."

"Good night, Ben."

Lying awake, going over tomorrow's strategies—anything was better than dreaming about Tony—a sudden thought stayed on to nag me . . . *the best laid plans of mice and men* . . .

Twenty-four

Tony Silva reappeared in my dreams and, perversely, I felt glad to see him. Thrilled, actually! Not me, I suppose—though it felt like me—but Karen, with her/my soul inside my/her body. He stroked my hair, gently twisting it through his long, lean brown fingers. The nails were square, cut short and immaculately clean. I reached up and pulled his head down, then kissed him. Tony's fingers left my hair and moved slowly down my body. As he reached my ankles, my toes twitched. I moaned, waking up Gypsy Rose.

She switched on the lamp, located in the center of the maple night stand between our twin beds. With her red curls tucked into some sort of frilly white sleep cap, she looked like a much foxier Martha Washington. "What's the matter, Jake?"

My travel alarm clock read three A.M. "Nothing. Just dreaming." I rolled over, anxious to return to Tony's arms.

But Gypsy Rose had a psychic moment. "It's Tony

Silva, isn't it?" She sighed. "Didn't I tell you that our dreams are not always what they seem? Go back to sleep."

I did, but the scene had changed. Music blared. I was in a pub, doing the twist with Andy Fielding. Greg Ford cut in. We danced till dawn.

. . . . .

Modesty, rising early, had walked to Fresh Fields in Georgetown—I'd bet they'd never seen the likes of her in that store—and bought "healthy whole wheat bagels and fat-free cream cheese for our breakfast." While Mom and Gypsy Rose attended to their toilettes, Aaron, Modesty, and I lingered over tea and bagels. After all, both bathrooms would be tied up during the ladies' lengthy reconstruction period.

When Mom had started dating Aaron, he'd been a three cups of coffee for breakfast man; his quick conversion to tea struck me as nothing short of a miracle. Modesty, too, drank the Lipton, with no complaints.

"Korea can be bitter cold," Modesty said. "My father had frostbite. Lost a toe, but gained a rank. Went from PFC to Corporal."

"Marine Corps?" Aaron frowned at his bagel. But then, how could a purist like him—"plain, please, smear of cream cheese"—be expected to enjoy a whole wheat bagel?

"Yes," Modesty said, ignoring his look of distaste. "He spent nine months there. My aunt Charity used to say that my father was never the same again. Of course, his tour of duty there came eons before my arrival, so I never quite knew what she meant."

I said, "Your dad died when you were very young, didn't he?"

"Yes." She doodled with her pen on a yellow pad. We writers always seemed to have a pad nearby. "I was three. He fell out of an apple tree on Aunt Charity's farm in Wisconsin. Broke his neck."

"My God, Modesty! I've never heard this story!" All the years I've known this woman and she's still an enigma.

"That's why I never eat apples. They're the root of all evil."

Aaron said, "I believe you're confusing apples with money."

"No!" Her voice rose. "Consider original sin! Not committed in the name of money, but for a bite of an apple! Taking that taste, Adam damned us all. Then, my father's ancestors had been Druids. Nature has always played a prominent role in a Druid's destiny. Dad had been doomed to drop from that tree."

Gypsy Rose, still wearing that silly cap, came into the dining room. "Jake, do you have toothpaste?" I wondered how a woman who'd carried a big black patent leather hatbox filled with creams and cosmetics aboard the shuttle could have forgotten her toothpaste.

"In my yellow case, on the dresser."

She started out of the dining room, then gave a start, and jerked back around, staring at Modesty. "Zelda says your father wants to reach you! Open your heart and mind this morning. We think he'll come through at the Korean Memorial!"

"How do you know it's my father?"

"Well, I didn't have to play Sherlock Holmes, darling!" Gypsy Rose chuckled. "Or even Dr. Watson! Zelda referred to the expected visitor from the world beyond as Harry Meade and said he wanted to chat with his daughter, Modesty. Don't you agree, chances are, that would be you?"

Modesty flushed. The rosy blush quickly spread from her brow to her chin, flooding her pale face with color. "Ooh! Yes!" Her voice quavered. "His name was Henry, but the family called him Harry!" She turned to me with what could almost pass for a smile. "Jake, did you hear that? My father's coming to Washington!"

God! With Modesty so thrilled, I hoped that Zelda hadn't been nipping at the gin.

Mom, her hair in Velcro curlers, but fully made-up, arrived at the table. "I'm so tired, Aaron didn't let me get to sleep till after two!"

Now my own brows flew up—higher and faster than hers ever had.

"So," Modesty said, "what were you guys doing till the wee hours of the morning?"

Giving a raucous laugh, Gypsy Rose departed. Aaron simply scratched his head.

Mom moved right along, ignoring all of our reactions. "But it was time well spent!" She deftly extracted a cell phone as tiny as Dennis's from a pocket in her beige linen jeans. "No bulge! Isn't that great? And isn't it cute? Aaron bought this for me yesterday, on our way back from chatting with Detective Wilson. I've never used one, you know. Now, after my middle of the night lessons, I've mastered all—well, most of—its mysteries. Watch!" She held her new toy aloft in the palm of her left hand, pressed a button, then smiled as my cell phone rang. "You're programmed, Jake. So is Aaron, Ben, Gypsy Rose, Modesty, Too Tall Tom, and even Greg Ford! If I need it, help is at my fingertips!"

I had to admit, I was impressed. I'd been after Mom to get a cell phone for years, but it took Aaron Rubin to convince her to put one in her pocket!

Finally, we were all fed and on our way. Mom and Modesty left first, heading over to the National

Cathedral. My mother, feeling a little jealous that Gypsy Rose and I had visited it without her yesterday, suggested stopping there, then taking the trolley tour that would drop them off at the Korean Monument.

Surprisingly, Modesty had agreed. "Why not? We can say a prayer there for my father. But first I want to call Rickie."

Then they'd gone out, arm in arm, discussing how their last stop would be the Smithsonian. Mom all smiles, telling Modesty, "Such a great gift shop!"

A taxi arrived to whisk Gypsy Rose away to Capitol Hill where Representative Barry Holstein would be conducting a private tour for her, including a visit to the House Chambers to watch the debate on the proposed trade bill, followed by lunch in a private, club-like dining room, where an ordinary citizen could only be fed if he or she were the guest of a senator or congressman. Would Andy Fielding be back here for that debate? Gypsy Rose might manage to chat with him.

As I watched her dramatic exit, wearing that cartwheel hat, a black and white linen dress with buttons up the back and a Sabrina neckline, and her scarlet toenails peeking out from strappy, high-heeled sandals, I figured she could lobby congress—successfully—for whatever the hell she wanted. Certainly poor old Barry Holstein wouldn't have a chance.

Aaron retreated to his bedroom to try and track down Ben. I hopped into the shower. One of my favorite places to think. All that warm water spraying down on my head stimulated my brain cells.

Several odd and seemingly unrelated things were bothering me. Karen Scanlon's family life for one. Why had she been such a free spirit? Most Irish Catholic girls raised in the 1950s and early 1960s would have been just the opposite. What had her mother been like? When had she been widowed? And how had her husband died? I scrunched my eyes shut to avoid being blinded by the shampoo and tried to visualize the dates on the Scanlon family tombstone. I didn't remember seeing Karen's mother's name. But hadn't Karen's father been buried there? How long before his wife and daughter had he died? I couldn't picture the names. And the photos I'd taken were in the drugstore in Carnegie Hill! Damn! Though it made no sense, I felt an overwhelming need to know. I'd call Timmy Rogers and have him check out the stone.

Then what about the aunt? Karen's only relative. Neither my computer search nor the NYPD had located a current address. Auntie had arranged for Karen's funeral and, apparently, vanished. Why? Would Detective Wilson know where she'd gone? Maybe she was dead, too. God knows, enjoying a long life span hadn't been a Scanlon family trait. Yet for no tangible reason, I felt certain I'd be meeting her.

Tony Silva and Clare Blake had vanished, too. Had that pop been a shot? Had he killed her? If not, what the hell had happened? And where were they now? With Father Blake's funeral mass scheduled for tomorrow, no way would his staid sister take off voluntarily.

Had Clare, despite her denial, known Tony back in the 1960s? I'd bet all of them had! The Fieldings, Ford, and even Billy Blake. Could Clare have been right? Had they conspired to protect Karen's murderer? Why would they do that? Clare told the police she'd been with her brother: To protect him or herself?

If they'd all known Tony back then, why hadn't anyone mentioned him to the police? Greg Ford and Andrew Fielding had been in love with Karen, for God's sake! According to Mrs. Carmody, Clare had been in love with Greg. She and Karen had quarreled over him on the morning of the murder. And Rebbeca frequently threw fits, screaming at Karen about Andy. Why would such feuding factions have been involved in a cover-up? What had been important enough to make them band together and lie like that? Or had only the killer lied, using—and somehow, tricking, deceiving—the others? Had the Fieldings and Ford really been together all evening? Had Clare and Billy Blake? And where had Tony been? Killing Karen? He'd certainly been in bed with her in my dreams. And there'd been a gun. God, had one or more of the friends hired him to murder Karen?

Or could I be back at square one?

Twenty-five

I thought I'd reintroduce Ed Wilson to Mrs. Carmody. They had a lot in common, and they'd make such a cute couple! Wilson reminded me of that old guy who owns the Wendy's fast-food chain and always stars in his company's TV commercials. Beats paying an actor! Same pudgy build, gray hair, and kind face. Same sort of sincerity that has sold millions of burgers.

Bright, avuncular, with a dry wit, and twinkling eyes. Plus Wilson also seemed to like Karen. If you can be said to like someone whom you only got to know after she was dead. God! Similar to my own situation!

Aaron, Ed, and I were having lunch at Billy Martin's. In Georgetown. I wondered which of its bar stools Mr. Carmody had decorated. I'd bet the saloon hadn't changed much since the 1960s.

A long bar covered the length of the left side of the room. Round tables in the middle created an airy, open look. And booths lined the pub's right wall. The restaurant was doing a thriving lunch business. Wilson had come early and had waited for us, sitting in a booth in the rear.

"Don't you believe for a minute that a stranger killed that poor girl. More likely a lover, certainly a friend!" Ed Wilson's large fist pounded on the table.

I asked, "What do you know about Tony Silva?"

"Until Aaron here mentioned his possible connection to the case yesterday, I only knew that Silva lobbied for the Intra-American Trade Association and, because I've kept up with the lives and times of my favorite suspects, Rebecca, Andy, Greg, Clare, and Father Blake, that he'd become acquainted with all of them."

"Did you really believe that Father Blake could have done it?"

"You bet! I never believed any of their alibis. I tell you, they were lying. Covering up. But I couldn't figure out why. It's been driving me crazy for thirty-four years."

"But Tony's name had never surfaced back in '67?"

"No, Jake. It sure didn't. Or, I promise you, I'd have hauled him in for questioning." Wilson stubbed out his cigarette in an ashtray that might have been hanging around since the 1960s.

"And did Clare Blake ever mention a Latin American Project?"

Wilson looked blank. "No, what's that?"

"Who, not what," I said. "On the phone yesterday, Clare Blake told me about Karen dating some guy and referring to him to as her 'Latin American Project.' "

"During the fatal phone call?"

"No, the call I'd taken earlier, at the airport."

Wilson blew smoke in my face. Maybe I'd been too quick to like this guy. "Now, let's see if I got this straight. Last evening, Clare called you a second time, then this Tony Silva shot her in the middle of the conversation. Is that right?" His tone indicated it couldn't be right. "Why would a smart guy like Tony do a thing like that?"

I had no answer. Hoping to think of one, I sipped my iced tea.

"Hit men don't like witnesses. Even audio witnesses." Wilson pulled another Chesterfield out of a crumpled pack. Damn! I'd probably leave here with nothing but a serious dose of secondary smoke damage.

I smiled as I asked, "Please, would you mind not smoking?"

"Yes." He lit the cigarette. I caught Aaron, sitting across from us, smirking.

Why hadn't I gone to the Korean War Veterans Memorial with Mom and Modesty?

"That thought has occurred to me, Detective Wilson," I said, sounding like a pompous ass, "and, you're right, Silva's shooting her then makes no sense; however, I believe that's exactly what happened."

Ed Wilson took a long drag, then exhaled in Aaron's direction, but said nothing.

"Look," I rambled on, "maybe he'd threatened Clare while she was dialing me, then when she started talking—she only said a few words—he shot her. Or, maybe, he'd been chasing her. She sounded out of breath. And then caught up to her, shooting, before he realized that she was on the phone . . ."

Wilson nodded. "That last one might fly. But how about this? What you heard wasn't a shot."

The waitress arrived with our cheeseburgers and, mercifully, Wilson put out his cigarette. I hoped he was a slow eater.

As he stacked his lettuce, tomato, raw onion, pickle, and a pile of cole slaw on one side of his bun, then added a quarter of a bottle of catsup to the other side, he said, "But don't worry, I've spent all of last night doing my homework on Anthony Silva. One hell of a guy!"

Ed Wilson's last words surprised and pleased me. I smiled and said, "Do tell, Detective!"

"Okay," he said between munches, "our boy arrives on a full scholarship to George Washington, provided by some Costa Rican charity whose records were all destroyed in a 1971 fire. That same year Tony gets his law degree from NYU. Cum laude. He'd been living in a furnished room on Broome Street. Paid his rent and his tuition in cash. Had no family listed on school records."

I asked, "His parents? What happened to them?"

"They were killed in an automobile accident in June of '65. In September, Tony came to the States as a student. All expenses paid by that mysterious Costa Rican charity. And Tony's not even Costa Rican. Well, he was born there . . ."

"Where were his parents from?"

"On his GW application, he'd listed his father's place of birth as Lisbon and his mother's as Berlin. They'd arrived in Costa Rica in '45. Right after Germany surrendered. Tony was born in '46. So he may have been Karen's Latin American Project, but he isn't really a Latino."

Truly amazing! I said, "You certainly have done your homework, pulling all this stuff together. And so fast. Better than the NYPD or the Justice Department. They haven't investigated Tony like this!"

Aaron frowned. "Don't be so certain about that, Jake. Last I heard, neither of those departments is obligated to report to you."

Wilson shrugged. "No big deal. I cashed in a few favors. Anyway, the first year that Tony attended NYU, he had no visible means of support. He worked as a law clerk for an international firm during his second and third summers. Went there full time when he graduated. Sharp negotiator. Started working for the Intra-American Trade Association four years later, 1975. Some political pundits claim Silva's long-term influence peddling has set our Latin America policy. He's mighty close to some big Latino businesses. God knows he's cozy with the Chairman of the Foreign Relations Committee, but that's been kept very low key. To quote some so-called sage, 'the Silva and Fielding relationship is no more than professional courtesy.' What BS! And, according to another of my sources, Tony's been banging Rebecca for years. And having long lunches with Greg Ford. I'd like to tap all of their goddamn phones."

I paused, with a French fry en route to my mouth. It could wait. "Wow! God, I am impressed. Thank you!" I dropped the fry back on the plate. "What about Karen's aunt? The one who buried her in Calvary? What became of her, Detective Wilson? Do you know?"

"I used to receive a Christmas card from her every year. She'd been working as a housekeeper, living in some rented room in South Jersey, when Karen had been killed . . ."

"I guess that's why the case didn't get much tabloid coverage in New York," I said.

"Yeah. Anyway, after a couple of years, my cards starting coming back. Agnes Scanlon had moved. No forwarding address. I never did find out where she'd gone."

I asked, "Who paid for Karen's funeral?"

"Greg Ford. Father Blake said the funeral mass at Georgetown. The entire Foreign Service School showed up. Very impressive. Then the five friends flew up to New York for the burial. Me, too. Wouldn't miss watching all those suspects in one place. You never saw so many graveside tears. Or so many flowers. Greg even sent a limo down to Red Bank to pick up Agnes." Wilson blew a perfect smoke ring. "The case still haunts me. That beautiful girl reminded me of my first love. Name of Jessie. Long dark hair and smooth white skin like Karen's. She died in a car accident when we were seventeen. I walked away from it. She went through the windshield."

I gulped. Had Karen once been Jessie? Jesus! Had I once been Jessie? I put down my cheeseburger. "Is that why you've remained so committed to solving this case?"

"Yeah. I guess so. That and the fact that I hate loose ends. The brass made me and my partner give up so early on—I've always wondered why. Always suspected something shady. The D.C. Police Department had more than a few . . ."

Aaron asked, "Do you believe there could have been a cover-up? Maybe a higher-up had been bribed? To sit on the case?"

Wilson lit still another Chesterfield. "That's my thinking, but I have no way of proving anything."

I finished my cheeseburger. It had grown cold while I'd been hanging on to Ed Wilson's every word. "Damn! Could Nicky Amas's death row—well, actually, pre-death row—confession have been the catalyst for Father Blake's murder after all? Had Cali ordered Silva to shoot Blake to keep him quiet? Has Cali been pulling the strings for over thirty-five years? Did he recruit Tony Silva way back in the mid-1960s, hiring him as a college hit man? Then plan Tony's career in international crime? Groom him as a front man for the Mexican drug cartel? Jeez, drugs weren't even that big a deal back then. Right?"

"All the more cunning," Aaron said.

Wilson exhaled, coughing. "That would explain how a poor student here on a scholarship wound up at NYU Law School, now wouldn't it?"

"Maybe not." I shook my head. "After all, how would a drug lord in Mexico know about a teenage orphan from Costa Rica?"

"I don't know," Wilson said, "but I sure as hell intend to find out!"

Twenty-six

One-thirty. We'd have to hustle our buns if we wanted to make that three o'clock shuttle. Mom had planned on all of us meeting at the National Airport at two. That wasn't going to happen.

Saying good-bye to Ed Wilson, I kissed one of his pudgy cheeks. "Thanks again. I'll be in touch!"

"I'll call you in New York," he said, the gruff voice mitigated by a clumsy hug.

Then Aaron and I grabbed a cab back to the Westchester, asking the driver to wait while we dashed into the lobby and picked up our luggage at the front desk. I took a lingering look at the lobby, suspecting that this be might be my last vestige of serenity for some time.

Traffic on Rock Creek Parkway seemed more like a morning commute crawl than a midday run to the airport. Could all these people be heading to National? We'd be lucky to arrive as our fellow shuttle passengers were boarding.

After checking our bags, searching for my ID, and

being ordered to dump out the entire contents of my tote as the metal detector had decreed, amazingly, Aaron and I were standing at the Delta ticket counter, picking up our boarding passes by two-thirty-five.

The waiting room was almost full, but Mom, Modesty, and Gypsy Rose were nowhere in sight. That feeling of your heart sinking to your stomach is not just a cliché; my heart definitely went on a downward spiral. "So where the hell are they?"

"God knows." Aaron seemed tired. Edgy. Fed up. No wonder. He'd paid his dues. Chasing down the bad guys—knowing he could be putting his fiancée's life in danger—should be behind him. With his exciting new career as a senator coming so late in life, he should be able to enjoy it, instead of racing around town playing Nancy Drew with his prospective stepdaughter.

"Let's sit for a minute," I said, "they'll show up."

We sank into seats, closer to the Boston gate than our own. If I closed my eyes, I'd probably fall asleep. I decided to take that chance.

I pushed B 9. The sound of "Strangers in the Night" filled the smoky room. Someone nuzzled my neck. God that felt good. A hazy pub slowly came into focus. Seedy. Smelling of stale cigarettes and strong booze. A sign above the old wooden bar read *Max's Pipe and Drum*. I raised my lips to be kissed. Tony Silva obliged. My toes tingled. Suddenly, Mom, looking decades younger, with long blonde hair, styled in a flip, stood at the bar. Tony turned from me, smiled at her, pulled a small gun from his jeans pocket, and shot. My mother fell . . .

The flight attendant's boarding announcement for the shuttle to La Guardia jerked me back awake. Surely only seconds could have passed.

I heard Gypsy Rose's high heels before I spotted her.

Coming at us from the rear, she shouted, "Jake, Aaron, hurry up, come get on line!" Then she circled round in front of our seats and waved us on.

Following her instructions and her hat, we obeyed. Still no sign of Mom and Modesty.

"Wait till you hear who showed up for lunch in the Capitol dining room!" No tired down time for Gypsy Rose. She positively sparkled.

Aaron asked, "Have you heard from Maura?"

The light in Gypsy Rose's eyes faded. "Oh God, isn't she here?"

As we all moved toward the gate, Aaron's and my cell phones rang at the exact same moment. He retrieved his faster than I did.

"We were getting worried, Maura," Aaron said. Judging by his smile, Mom must be okay. My heart lurched back in place.

My caller was Timmy Rogers. "Hi," I said. "We're just about ready to board the shuttle."

"You're on the escalator now?" Aaron said.

"I have those dates you wanted," Timmy said.

"Huh?" Still thinking about Tony Silva and my mother, I had no idea what Timmy was talking about.

"You know from the headstone on the Scanlon grave."

"Right! Thanks! Go ahead, Timmy."

Aaron said, "Hurry up, Maura. We're ready to roll. Yes. I'll ask them to hold the plane." He laughed. "But I wouldn't count on it! So you and Modesty had better move it. Climb, don't ride those steps!"

"Her father died in 1951," Timmy said. "In Korea."

Had everyone's father fought in America's "forgotten" war? I sighed. "And Karen's mother? What about her?"

Gypsy Rose asked, "Can I speak to Maura?"

"No! For God's sake," Aaron said, "she'll be here any second!"

The flight attendant took my boarding pass, tore off the main portion, and handed me the stub. "Thank you for flying Delta."

Instead of entering the corridor leading to the plane, I stepped over to one side, joining Aaron and Gypsy Rose, who were waiting for my mother. Only two other passengers were still in line. "Sorry, Timmy, I didn't hear you . . ."

He said, "Karen's mother, nee Maria Montez, died on December 16, 1966. About seven months before her daughter."

Maria Montez? Had Karen's mother been Mexican? "Timmy, where . . ." My cell phone sputtered, then static filled my ear. I'd lost Timmy.

Mom and Modesty running, out of breath but full of apologies, reached us just as the flight attendant was about to shut down her station and close up the entrance way to the plane.

"Goddamn!" I shoved the phone back in my bag. My mother gave me a dirty look.

Aaron and Mom found two empty seats together in the last row. He had been clinging to her arm and whispering in her ear since she'd arrived. Modesty sat across the aisle and one row in front of me. Gypsy Rose now had the middle seat between an overweight man and a surly teenage boy. The man's briefcase had been occupying the seat, but Gypsy Rose had moved it onto his stomach. He wasn't happy. I wound up wedged between an old man who seemed to have forgotten how to smile, and a stunning young woman who never stopped.

The steward announced that all cell phones had to be turned off. I'd planned on using Mom's new mini. Instead, as soon as the steward gave the okay, I called

Timmy on the in-plane phone located in the back of the seat in front of me. Talk about static. But we were connected.

"Jake, I can hardly hear you . . ."

"Where was Karen's mother born?" I shouted, now getting a nasty look from the old guy in the window seat. "Mexico?"

"Trenton. Last I heard that would be in New Jersey."

"Damn!"

"Why? What difference does it make?"

"Just a wild card hunch. Forget about it. Hey, Timmy, thanks!"

"My pleasure. Now one other thing. You'd mentioned that you were looking for Karen's aunt . . . could her name be Agnes Scanlon?"

"Yes!"

"I stopped by the office at Calvary. Guess who's paying for perpetual care on the Scanlon family grave site?"

"Aunt Agnes!"

"Is that your final answer?" Timmy laughed. "And now for the bonus round . . ."

"Timmy!"

"Okay, okay. Agnes Scanlon is alive and well, living in Southampton. Write down this address and phone number."

I dug in my tote for paper and pen. "Bless you, Timmy!"

As the steward served the cute little Delta Shuttle basket, containing a dwarf apple, a bite-size piece of processed cheese, two really small crackers, a miniature Milky Way, a teeny blue and white paper napkin, a little bitty plastic knife, and a bone dry Wash-up "moist" towelette, I asked for a coffee—suddenly, craving caffeine. And stared at the address. Dune Road, Southampton. Well, well. Aunt Agnes must have come into some money!

Twenty-seven

Modesty had driven to the airport yesterday afternoon, leaving her VW in long-term parking. Though Mom, Gypsy Rose, and Aaron made it clear that they'd prefer to grab a cab, she insisted all four of us squeeze into the Beetle for the ride back to Manhattan.

You can't win when Modesty's really determined. She pulled goggles out from her J. Peterman duster's pocket and, looking eerily like a turn-of-the-last-century Model T driver, slid behind the wheel. Aaron stashed Mom's midsize bags in the tiny trunk, then climbed into the front passenger seat. Mom, Gypsy Rose, and I wound up squashed in the back seat, with too many totes and shopping bags piled on our laps and spilling over onto our feet.

Aaron clutched the dashboard as Modesty sped out of the Marine Air terminal and onto the Brooklyn–Queens Expressway. A major misnomer. We all knew that the traffic from Long Island would slow her down before we hit the toll booth. Or maybe not. She weaved the

Bug through any possible openings and forged holes where there were none.

But all this togetherness gave us a chance to share our morning adventures. I let Aaron tell our tale.

"Well," my mother said as Aaron finished, "I'm relieved to hear that; at least, Ed Wilson is investigating Tony Silva."

Aaron frowned. "Clare Blake has only been out of touch since late yesterday afternoon," he looked at his watch, "barely twenty-four hours."

I suppressed a very real desire to slap my future stepfather. "Out of touch? For God's sake, Aaron, she'd been trying to tell me something about Tony Silva, then I heard a shot. Now no one, including the NYPD, can find either of them. I'd say that adds up to more than being out of touch!"

"There's no hard evidence. Nothing that directly connects Silva to Cali, but I'm sure Ben's checking him out. Most cops don't talk about what they're doing, you know." Testy. Mom's and my implied disapproval of his son's lack of detective work seemed to have offended Aaron's pride in the Rubin family's long history of successful police investigations.

Gypsy Rose changed the subject. "To continue with the thought that simply flew right of my head back there at National when I'd realized Maura had gone missing . . ."

"What about me?" Modesty asked. "Weren't you worried about me? I'd gone missing, too."

"Of course, darling," Gypsy Rose said, "though I didn't sense any danger for you . . ."

"But you sensed danger for me," my mother said, "didn't you?"

Gypsy Rose hesitated. It didn't take psychic ability for me to sense that she'd been caught in a New Age ethical quandary—wanting to tell the truth, but not wanting her slip of the tongue to scare her friend. She opted for the former, "Yes. I did. And, Maura, you really need to stay on guard till this killer is arrested."

Mom nodded. "I know. The FBI must think so, too. I spotted a tail."

More than I'd been able to do.

Gypsy Rose said, "You see. It all became clear during the main course."

Somehow I'd missed a segue. I wasn't alone. Aaron asked her, "What the hell are you talking about?"

"Danger," Gypsy Rose said, "in the dining room at the Capitol. During the main course. Salmon. Poached, with a wonderful cream sauce. I heard machine gun fire."

I felt my mouth drop open. My mother's eyes grew wide and she took my hand. Modesty swerved to the right, then passed an angry taxi driver. Aaron stiffened, but didn't turn around. He watched the road. Intently. I'd bet he was wishing he could wrest that wheel from Modesty.

"Machine gun fire?" I asked.

"Suddenly the dining room became freezing cold. Then this young man—though not as young as the others—wearing a Marine uniform, snow on his shoulders, appeared before me."

Aaron, still staring straight ahead, asked, "What did Congressman Holstein have to say about your visitors?"

"I said they appeared to me." Gypsy Rose spoke softly, but with unwavering conviction.

Modesty asked, "What time did this vision occur?"

"Just before noon. I remember Barry joking about our eating so early, saying how we never have lunch before one in Manhattan." Gypsy Rose touched Modesty's shoulder. "Why do you ask?"

"Because my father never showed up at the Korean Memorial. And you said he would!" Modesty turned around to confront Gypsy Rose. Aaron grabbed the wheel. "And then," Modesty continued, "just when Maura had said, 'It's almost noon, we should have some lunch,' I felt really cold—freezing—and I swear I heard shooting—shots—ratta-tat-tat shots. Now, what I'd like to know is why did my father appear to you instead of visiting his own daughter?" She swung back around and shoved Aaron's hand off the wheel.

Gypsy Rose smiled. "Darling, sometimes the spirits in the world beyond, like the rest of us, get their signals crossed." I watched Aaron shake his head. "Like they know they're supposed to make an appearance in Washington, but they show up at the wrong place."

"So my father . . ."

"I'm sure your father was present, Modesty, but he never spoke to me. Probably he'd been very disappointed that he'd missed you! No, the Marine who passed a message on to me was the spirit of Karen Scanlon's father."

"And what did he say?" I asked.

"Haven't I been telling you? He said to warn Maura. And that Karen's murder had to be avenged!"

My mother smiled. "Jack came through, too, didn't he? He had to be one of them! I felt that chill. And heard those same shots. Doesn't surprise me that those Marines landed at the wrong place. In all the years I was married to Jack O'Hara, he never could follow directions!"

Gypsy Rose laughed. "You're so right. Oh—one more thing—Barry Holstein said that no committee meeting had been scheduled yesterday. And a clerk in Andrew Fielding's office mentioned that his boss had flown back to Manhattan. Supposedly to see his wife. Now let me get back to Sergeant Scanlon's spirit . . ."

Aaron said, "Modesty, you'd better move over a lane, or you'll miss the Ninety-sixth Street exit!"

. . . . .

By six o'clock, Modesty and I sat at one of Vico's outdoor tables, sipping cosmopolitans, and waiting for Jane, Too Tall Tom, and Dennis to join us. Mom and Gypsy Rose had squirreled in and would be spending the evening together. Aaron had gone down to the police station to "see how I can help Ben."

Three tables to our east, a good-looking, youngish guy in conservative threads and shades sat watching my co-op. Mom's FBI tail, I presumed.

"I'm only here because of your mother," Modesty said, "the last thing I need is another dose of Jane's venom. And I want to see Rickie. We've never spent a night apart before. I missed sleeping with him!"

These sparsely scattered romantic revelations never ceased to surprise me. Who'd have ever thought that Modesty could be capable of such passion? She sounded like a woman in the throes of her first love affair. Maybe she was.

"Actually, much as I hate to ruin your rendezvous, I want to see Rickie, too. Maybe we can all have dinner together."

"Yeah. I thought you would." Modesty twisted a plastic stirrer. "I listened to Aaron's end of that conversation with Ben, too. Sounded like your boyfriend still hasn't gotten a search warrant for Silva's apartment."

"Right!" I sighed. "And, for a change, he'd been way too busy to talk to me." Jeez, girl talk. Exchanging confidences about the men in our lives! If Jane could only hear us now!

"Modesty, did you sleep in that duster?" Jane appeared at my side. Damn! She probably had overheard!

Impeccable, as always. Why didn't linen wrinkle on this woman? Dressed in a crisp, ankle-length, gray linen sheath, with matching slides, and carrying a small, darker gray tote bag, Jane made me feel grimy. I don't know how she made Modesty feel, but I'd bet we were in for a rocky cocktail hour.

"Hi!" Too Tall Tom yelled, waving wildly, as he dashed across Madison Avenue. I've never appreciated his timing or his enthusiasm more. I'd just let him do most of the talking.

After flirting with the waiter, while ordering Jane's white wine spritzer and his own iced tea, he said, "Can you stand it? I have to go back to work for the bitch tonight!" Then he rummaged through his Tiffany day planner.

Jane said, "What are you looking for?"

"My business cards. I want to give one to that charming young man." Flipping pages, he shouted, "Voila!"

"Did anything happen today at 1040 Fifth?" I asked.

"My dear," he said, "such goings on!"

"So tell us," Modesty snapped. Good. Better to vent than to sulk. Even if an innocent man had to take the brunt of her anger.

"Well, no phone calls from Tony today. Has he turned up anywhere?"

"No!" Modesty and I shouted.

"But, while Madam lunched at Le Cirque with none other than Greg Ford, I read her e-mail!"

"You broke into her computer?"

"Very simple. Her password is 'money.' " Too Tall Tom laughed. "Took me just three tries to find it. People do save the damnedest things. And the lady is a tramp. I'm telling you her love-mail to and from Tony is torrid. Details of graphic sex in the strangest spots! Heating up cyberspace, darlings!"

"What website would that be?" Dennis Kim had arrived.

When Dennis's martini had been served and Too Tall Tom had slipped his card to the waiter, Modesty asked for my cell phone and wandered off with it. No doubt calling Rickie to arrange our caper. Since she was standing on the sidewalk, straight in front of the suspected FBI agent's nose, I hoped he couldn't read lips.

Too Tall Tom pulled some papers out of his planner. "Copies of Rebecca's e-mail love letters!"

I said, "You're wonderful!"

"Aren't I though?" He beamed. "And, to light a fire under his fanny, I've dropped copies of all this hot stuff at Ben Rubin's office!"

Jane said, "Yes, yes. Congratulations, Too Tall Tom, but I have news, too!"

Modesty returned, giving me a thumbs up.

Jane plowed on, "I interviewed Andrew Fielding in person. We had tea at the St. Regis. He explained what he was doing in New York yesterday, how he'd left Washington, unexpectedly. You see, he knew that Clare Blake was staying at the Barbizon and, with his committee meeting canceled, he'd decided to pay a condolence call. But she'd gone out. All very plausible. You can scratch him off your list of suspects, Jake. He's just way too charming to have killed anyone!"

I had to physically restrain Modesty.

Too Tall Tom said, "All things considered, Jane, I

liked you better when you had less style and more brains."

Dennis laughed, but Jane leapt up and stomped off, saying, "I'm out of here. The rest of you ghosts can sit around and play Clue with Perry Mason, but I have more important things to do!"

Damn! I called after her, "Jane . . . I'll talk to you in the morning!"

She never looked back.

Dennis drained his glass, "Don't worry, Jake, she'll get over it. How about joining me for dinner?"

Too Tall Tom stood. "Thanks, but unfortunately, I have to go back to my moldings. Maybe I can squeeze in some more snooping." He turned to me. "Dennis is right, Jake. Jane's mad now, but after a trip to Bloomies, she'll be herself again. God help us all."

"So, what do you say, ladies? Dinner at Elaine's?"

"Sorry, Dennis, I promised Modesty I'd . . ."

"Help me edit my book!" Modesty jumped up.

"A noble undertaking!" Dennis knew damn well that Modesty's Gothic mystery novel had been edited to death and still ran over 2,000 pages. "Please, whatever you two are up to, try not to get arrested."

Twenty-eight

Dennis paid the bill, then walked us to the Beetle. I needed a favor, but since we'd just lied to him—and he knew it—I felt somewhat hesitant about asking for a ride out to Southampton tomorrow.

Modesty groused about Jane from 92nd and Madison to 91st, just west of Park, where she'd parked the car. Dennis and I said nothing.

Opening the passenger door for me, Modesty asked Dennis, "Are you going to Father Blake's funeral in the morning?"

"Yes. Billy Blake was a great guy. I've blocked out a couple of hours, so I can attend his mass."

I gulped. Now or never. "We might do him more good by skipping his funeral and driving out to Southampton."

"Realizing that logic has never been your strong suit, Jake, I feel compelled to ask how and why you've come to that conclusion."

"Logic has nothing to do with it!"

He laughed. "I'll bet."

"Listen to me, Dennis!" I had one hand on the VW door and the other gripping his arm. Modesty sat in the driver's seat, waiting. "Timmy Rogers located Agnes Scanlon, Karen's aunt and only living relative. Even if you don't accept the premise that Karen and I share the same soul, believe that I believe it." He stared at me. Puzzled? Worried? "Well, I almost believe it!" I raised my voice. "And deep in the recesses of my—our—soul, I sense that Agnes Scanlon holds the key to this mystery. I must talk to this woman!"

He bent and kissed my forehead. "Okay. Okay. We'll go to Southampton in the morning. But we'll have to leave at six. Be ready! I have a meeting tomorrow afternoon at two that I can't miss. Looks like I might have a publisher for Greg Ford's book."

Modesty pulled out from the curb with a vengeance. "Are you really going to miss a funeral?"

"What do you mean?"

"Lately, I've been thinking of you as a Junior Ms. version of Mrs. McMahon. That attending funerals had become your avocation. Never to be missed affairs. And here you are taking a pass."

Could she be kidding? But Modesty never joked. Jeez, had I gone from ghost to ghoul? I sighed. "I guess you're right. Too many wakes? Too many memorials? Too many requiems?"

"Yeah. I'd suggest a moratorium."

I phoned Mom from the VW. "Don't stay up waiting for me. I'm having dinner at Modesty's, then I'm going out with her and Rickie." True enough.

"Good. You deserve to have some fun!" A sharp prick attacked my conscience. I tried to ignore it. "Jake, Aaron just called. Nick Amas died earlier this afternoon."

Now wasn't that convenient for the killer? "Did he

say anything before he died?" A long shot, but something villains frequently do in the movies.

"No deathbed confession. He never woke up." Mom sighed. "One other thing, don't plan on attending Father Blake's funeral. It's by invitation only. Mine came today."

"You can't go alone!"

"Aaron's going with me. Greg Ford asked him to attend."

"Okay, I'd made other plans for tomorrow anyway. Dennis is going with me to interview Karen's aunt Agnes. You and Gypsy Rose have a good night. We'll catch up in the morning."

. . . . .

The smell of basil greeted us. Once again, I marveled at Modesty's apartment. The decor, a charming mix of merry olde England, a bit of whimsy, and a hint of Martha Stewart, made me smile. Lots of crystal, fresh flowers, and quaint old claret velvet chairs, tempered by touches of white enamel and silk. All reinforcing my theory that under Modesty's miserable exterior beat the heart of a happy woman. And one who'd been happy even before a man had appeared on the scene.

The man in question, Rickie Romero, had pasta, homemade Italian bread, and iced tea ready to serve when we arrived.

"Ciao, bella Jake," he said, kissing me on both cheeks. "No vino for you ladies tonight? The cat and his kittens must be in primo form."

I thought—not for the first time—that the retired burglar, with Fabio's looks, had to be one of the most attractive men in New York City and also one of the most annoying. How the hell had this odd couple lived together for three months? Way too good sex had to be the answer.

While Modesty fussed in the kitchen, Rickie and I sat at the antique table and watched the lights of the city flickering through the glass door leading to the balcony.

"Modesty called me from D.C. last night and alerted me to the possibility of a visit to Tony Silva's." Rickie passed the pasta. "So I did a run through around three o'clock this morning."

I remembered how easily he'd vanished over the balcony the last time I'd been here. Of course, at that moment, he'd been my prime suspect. Now I'd be his accomplice. "I—er—have some misgivings. You're retired now—I don't want to be responsible for your resuming . . ."

"A life of crime? Bella, we're only going on a reconnaissance mission, not a robbery."

"Well, I suppose, technically, that's true. But legally, it's still breaking and entering, isn't it?"

He chuckled, "Only if we get caught!"

The terror in my heart must have broken out all over my face. Rickie smiled and leaned closer to me. "I promise you we won't be caught."

Modesty came in from the kitchen with the bread basket. He took it from her, placed it on the table, and pulled her on his lap. She brushed her lips against his cheek. Watching Modesty as a femme fatale proved to be a delightful diversion, and my heart fell back in place.

Rickie said, "I'm taking a real job, Jake. Did you know that?"

"No. Doing what?"

"Head of security." He grinned. "At Tiffany's."

Like a sneeze you can't control, like that wave in *The Perfect Storm*, like the iceberg in *Titanic*, hysterical laughter consumed me.

"While I see the irony, too," he said, "it's really not that funny, Jake. Don't you think that the man who once stole the Faith Diamond would be the best man to protect Tiffany's?"

Still unable to speak, I nodded.

"And I need the income. They pay well—not up to my former standard of living—but enough. Did Modesty tell you that we're getting married? We hope to have many babies."

Another wave swept over me. One of pure, unadulterated jealousy. First Mom. Now Modesty. I'll be the old maid. The one whom everyone will feel obligated to invite for Sunday dinners. Without even making an attempt to offer congratulations, I fled to the bathroom.

What the hell has happened to me? I've never had designs on marriage. To the contrary, for years, I've espoused the joys of single blessedness. And, if I wanted to be married, Dennis had made an offer. The trouble was I didn't know what I wanted. Could I be having a midlife crisis? Ahead of schedule. God, I'd just turned thirty-four. How batty would I be by forty?

I splashed cold water on my face. Could I really be in love with two men? Maybe I didn't know what love was. Did anyone? Could this case be the problem? I hadn't been getting enough sleep, I'd been scared to death about Mom's safety, sometimes I believed that Karen had taken over my mind as well as my soul, and I was about to commit a felony. No wonder I felt crazy. Just get on with it, Jake!

When I returned to the table, Modesty had filled my plate. "Sorry, guys, I felt a little woozy there. Not enough sleep." I sat down, suddenly starving. "So what are we going to do while we wait until dark?"

Rickie smiled. "Rehearse. Rehearse. Then rehearse some more."

While we had our coffee—"just one cup, I don't want you kittens to be edgy"—he spread out photographs, a hand-drawn map, and the floor plan of Tony Silva's home on the table. The man had been busy.

"Where is this building?" I asked.

"On your turf. Carnegie Hill," Rickie said. "South side of 94th Street, between Fifth and Madison. Very impressive, an old brownstone. Built around 1900. And, when so many townhouses were becoming co-ops after the war, this one remained a private home. I knew that he referred to WW II, despite all the wars since then. "Tony Silva has five floors of living space. Such decadence!"

I stared at the photo of the solid stone house; it looked like a fortress. "How in God's name are we going to get in?"

Modesty said, "Rickie's been waiting all day to answer that question."

Twenty-nine

This caper's choreography had to rival *A Chorus Line*'s. Rickie hadn't missed a beat. Not even with wardrobe.

Modesty would be our lookout. Dressed as a bag lady, she'd take up her position across the street from Silva's townhouse, on the steps leading down to Ramakrishna Vivekananda, Swami Adiswarananda's stone temple. A match made in heaven—the temple was one of Carnegie Hill's many multicultural religious centers and Modesty was a nondenominational Druid.

Rickie had considered the International Center for Photography, my favorite museum, but its doorway had no depth. At the temple—where a prominent sign proclaimed All Are Welcome—she could squat in comfort.

If the cops questioned her, she'd react like a street person, who'd bedded down there for the night. Indignant at being asked to move. Defying authority. Slightly batty. Her eyes lit up as Rickie gave directions. She'd been born to play this role.

And her costume was divine. A ratty monk's robe, basic black, that she'd developed an attachment to and refused to throw away. Rickie had found it in her closet. He'd cut the hem into tatters and stained the front with catsup and mustard. She smelled like a deli sandwich.

But he'd gone too far, cutting holes in her black high tops. Examining a painted toe nail, poking through one of the holes, she said, "Damn it, Rickie, these sneakers were new!"

He handed her a Harpo Marx wig. "We must suffer for our art, Modesty!" With black grease streaking her cheeks and her two top front teeth painted out, I'd have given her a handout.

I, too, got to wear a wig. Long and black, styled in pigtails. Morticia goes to Oz. But I loved my costume. Rickie had gone shopping in the Village. Black tights, black turtleneck, very Audrey Hepburn, too heavy for June. I didn't balk, not wanting to hear his sacrifice shtick again. Shoes that looked like robust black ballet slippers. Size seven. Too tight, but, unlike Cinderella's stepsisters, I squeezed into them. When he added black harlequin glasses, I didn't recognize myself. However, I still wasn't sure exactly what part I'd be playing.

Rickie wore a gray and black checkerboard pattern shirt and dark gray, loose-fitting pants. His shoes, like mine, resembled ballet slippers, with sticky rubber soles. "Providing both friction and a silent climb!" He placed a silk hood around his neck like a dickey, then pulled it up to cover his mouth and nose, obviating the need for camouflage face paint.

One of my props was a plastic doggie poop bag. "Why am I carrying this?"

Rickie laughed. "Well, if the cops stop you and ask what you're doing roaming around Carnegie Hill streets at two A.M., you can say you're looking for your dog.

You'd arrived home late, taken him for a walk, and he'd run away."

"In this outfit?"

"Get in character, Jake! This is the way Totsie Tooter dresses!"

"Totsie Tooter?"

"That's your role. Now act the part!"

Once we were all in our costumes, Rickie set the stage. "I think of this as my final caper! You're both writers; think about how excited you feel when you're about to write your final chapter. Reach for and use that emotion. Elation equals energy! Have fun with this! A happy thief finds the jewels!"

Since Modesty's book now had ninety-two chapters, with no end in sight, and I hadn't even begun to write my own murder mystery, this final chapter/caper attitude would require some real acting ability!

"Listen, Rickie, you're dealing with two ghostwriters here."

"A ghost today, a bestseller tomorrow." He smiled. "Now let's go over the action. Actually, this should be a breeze. A waste of this cat's talent."

Confidence or arrogance? "How's that?"

"First, I'm extremely well prepared. I enacted a complete dress rehearsal last night. Spidermanned my way up the apartment house on the corner of Madison and Ninety-fourth, used ten-millimeter-wide rope, securing it to a post on the roof, and rappelled down to the townhouse roof next door. Worked my way across the rooftops to Silva's, and jimmied a bedroom window, despite the best security system that money can buy—to prove I could do it in under two minutes. Then I went back down on the outside of Silva's building just like Santa. His townhouse is an old Victorian, designed with cement slabs. Very convenient for my line of work. Built-in steps."

"Rickie's the very best burglar in the world!" Modesty sounded like the proud mother of a six-year-old boy.

"I'm a regular at the photography museum, so I've passed that apartment house on the corner of Ninety-fourth and Madison hundreds of times. Its front is covered with fire escapes. Why didn't you climb up one of them?"

His look of disdain disarmed me. "Are you mad? I'm an artist, not some punk kid doing my first B and E the easy, sloppy way! No cat burglar who takes any pride in his work be so amateurish! Rattle the metal and some-one will see or hear you on a fire escape!"

"Well, I'd like to try it the easy, sloppy way! Can I use the fire escape?"

"No! You're not climbing anything! I'll go through the top-floor window, down the inside hall stairs, and open the front door for you."

Timing, Rickie explained, was everything. We syn-chronized our watches and rehearsed our movements minute by minute—every action accounted for, includ-ing a contingency plan and an emergency escape route.

Then we all put on our plastic gloves and went to work!

．．．．．

New York may be the city that never sleeps, but at two A.M., the residents of 94th Street, between Fifth and Madison, seemed to be in dreamland.

Modesty and I had walked up Park. She, a half block ahead of me so, if spotted, no one would think we were together. As coached, I acted distraught, clutching my pooper-scooper bag to my chest. But, except for two late-niters, who had exited taxis in front of their Park

Avenue canopies and their respective doormen, I'd seen no one.

Rickie had left earlier, running along Lexington. Exercise nuts jog at all hours. Even if people took notice of him, they probably wouldn't recall any details. He'd be dismissed as just another crazy jogger.

Now, halfway up the block, heading west, the silence struck me as eerie. I chuckled; no audience needed for this performance.

Modesty had assumed her position in front of the temple. I glanced at my watch. Two-two. Rickie should be arriving in Silva's lobby in one minute. Then I glanced, once again, across the street, where Modesty sat in cross-legged comfort on the top step.

Suddenly, I spied a patrol car, turning left off Fifth, cruising down the block. Its headlights coming straight at me. Almost at Silva's house, I had nowhere to hide!

Jesus, Mary, and Joseph! The cops pulled up alongside Modesty!

I ducked behind a skinny little city tree that didn't even cover my butt, as my leap-frogging heart dropped to somewhere around my ovaries. I strained, but couldn't hear what the officer said to her. I could only pray she'd remember her lines.

Then I heard her. Brassy, bold, beautiful. "This here's a free country, ain't it? I don't tell you where you to sleep, don't you dare tell me where I can sleep. Them park benches are too full of splinters for my sensitive skin."

The cop said something in reply.

Modesty screamed, "Go away, fascist!"

And, unbelievably, after they exchanged a few more words, that I couldn't hear, he did. But for how long?

Modesty's rants and raves as the patrol car drove away answered my question. "Whether you cops come

back in fifteen minutes or fifteen years, I'll still be here!
I'm not going anywhere!"

I ran the short distance to Silva's house and sprinted
up the stoop. Rickie opened the door before I hit the top
step. But the terror stayed with me, clinging like an
albatross around my neck, and causing sweat to drip
down from under my wig. I wanted to peel off the
turtleneck.

We had less than fifteen minutes to search the
apartment and make our getaway!

The foyer had white marble walls and floors and a
twelve-foot ceiling, with a marvelous, old chandelier,
shining brightly. Too bright for me! "Shouldn't we turn
that off?"

"No! The hall light is left on all night." Rickie spoke
in low, firm tones. "Now be quiet. Take the stairs to the
top floor." He propped the heavy oak front door open,
using a tiny metal wedge he pulled out of his pocket.
"They lead directly into Silva's library. Let's start
there."

"Where are you going?"

"To get Modesty before the cops come back. We'll
meet you up there. Here—" he handed me a tiny flash-
light—"get going. This operation took longer than I'd
planned. No time to look around." He waved a hand.
Imperiously. "Move it, Jake. We don't have all night!"

Large floor-to-ceiling white double doors were on my
right as I started up the steps, partially covered in Persian
carpeting. Bet they entered into a grand salon. Well, if
I hurried, I'd get to see it on the way out. The dark
wooden banisters and floors were magnificent. If only
I'd been a guest, not a burglar, I could savor all these
great touches.

On the third-floor landing, I noticed an open door,
leading into what appeared to be a sitting room. Good

God! Could that be a woman's leg draped over the arm of the royal blue velvet settee?

Should I disobey Rickie and take a detour? Could I really have gone mad?

Hell, I'll just sneak a peek. Be in and out in a second. He'll never even know.

The enormous room's ornate ceiling, featuring angels and cherubs, had to be even higher than twelve feet. The settee faced a black marble fireplace. Long past the last blaze of winter, its leftover ashes gave off a sooty smell. I inched closer.

Clare Blake's very dead body sprawled, indecorously, all over the love seat.

Thirty

I was still screaming when Modesty and Rickie came running into the room.

"Shut up, Jake!" Focusing on me, he didn't notice Clare's leg.

But Modesty did. She strode across the room and stood next to me in front of the settee. "My God, Clare Blake's been shot in the head!"

Her shout, overpowering my screams, propelled Rickie forward. After a quick look at the corpse, he took action. Placing one arm around Modesty's shoulders and the other around mine, he spoke in a kinder, gentler, almost soothing tone. "Pull yourselves together, kittens. We have work to do before we can call the police."

"The police?" Modesty shrieked. "Why would we do that? Haven't I spent most of my time tonight trying to avoid them? Followed by that mad dash across the street, sneaking into the house so they wouldn't see us!"

Rickie flashed his amazingly attractive smile at Modesty. "An anonymous 911 call, darling. Like any good citizen would make. But not till we're finished here."

I swallowed back another scream and took a deep breath. "Silva must have killed her! Do you think he's in the house, hiding somewhere?"

Modesty stared at the open door, as if expecting our missing host to walk in any moment.

Rickie said, "I wouldn't worry about that. Silva knows the police will arrive on the scene. And soon. He's probably south of the border by now."

I felt totally helpless. And I came across that way, too. "So what are we going to do?"

Rickie squeezed my shoulder, then removed his arm. "What we came to do. Look for Karen's picture and the safe supposedly behind it. We could crack this case before Ben Rubin gets a search warrant!"

Deciding not to separate, we started our hunt on the top floor. The extensive library looked like a set design from *Pygmalion*, only this Higgins seemed to have never read any of his books. Or written a note. Or sat at his desk. Not a thing was out of place. I marveled at how quickly—and neatly—Rickie ripped through the room, missing nothing, but putting everything back in the same perfect order. No one would ever know that we'd been here.

The guest bedrooms and baths reflected that same super neat, compulsive method of housekeeping. Silva must have the best help in Manhattan. Where in the world did he find his maids?

Then, in the master bedroom, we struck pay dirt! The room had been ransacked. By a dedicated—or a desperate—professional! All the drawers and closets had been emptied. Clothes, jewelry, cash, papers, books, magazines, CDs, linens, and empty boxes were scattered wall-to-wall. A briefcase, sliced up into small strings of leather, lay forlorn in a corner. The bed had been stripped and the mattress cut open, its stuffing strewn about on the Oriental rug.

A poster-size photograph of Karen Scanlon, hanging over Tony's bed, had not been moved. Or marred. A small table, directly below the picture, held a crystal bowl of white roses, only slightly wilted. The roses, too, had been left in place. Weird. Why?

Rickie lifted the picture off the wall. No safe. Somehow, I wasn't surprised.

Modesty asked, "Why would Silva trash his own bedroom? Anyone as anal retentive as this guy would be able to find his stuff—at all times."

Rickie and I shook our heads.

"He didn't do this, did he?" Modesty's pale green eyes darkened. "Maybe Tony isn't our killer?"

"He might have a bullet in his brain, too," Rickie said.

I shuddered. "And his body could be in any one of this mansion's many rooms."

Modesty asked, "I'd rather get out of here right now, but should we start searching the other floors?"

Checking his watch, Rickie said, "We're already behind schedule!"

She started to remove one of her plastic gloves.

"Don't take that off, Modesty," Rickie said, "you'll leave DNA behind."

"Okay! Okay!" She raised her voice. I suspected the cat was getting on more than one of his kittens' nerves. "If Tony Silva isn't our boy, who is?"

I said, "We have plenty of other suspects to select from."

Rickie smiled. "The prospect of the United States Attorney of the Southern District of New York being a multiple murderer tickles my whiskers. However, I'd settle for that cracker congressman, Randy Andy Fielding. He's such a lecher, he deserves the chair."

When had Romero turned into such a moral judge and jury? By his standards, half the men I've dated deserved to die. Then again, maybe he had a point.

"Too Tall Tom thinks it's Rebecca Sharpe-Fielding," Modesty said. "I never did like that woman."

I laughed. Loudly. What a hoot! As if she'd ever liked any female. Well, except for Mom, Gypsy Rose, and me. And, based on the nasty look she just gave me, I wasn't so sure about me.

"Damn! Once again, we're back where we started," I said. "Cali could be the killer. And all this Karen Scanlon business—connecting the dots to tie Father Blake's death to a thirty-four-year-old murder—could be only in my dreams!"

A police siren's wail—close by—made the three of us jump.

"Let's get out of here," Rickie said, shutting off the light. "I'll go out the same window I came in. Scale that brick house right across the back alley and land on Ninety-third Street. Then I'll head south on Madison.

"You and Modesty take the stairs down, go out the front door. Exit one at a time. Modesty first. Be sure to take off your Harpo wig, before you leave the foyer. Check for cops. Walk right to Madison. Cross the avenue, head straight over to Third, before going south."

The siren ceased. We were—temporarily—in the clear.

Rickie continued. "Jake, walk to Fifth; go north for a block, turn east on Ninety-fifth to Lexington; then south to Ninety-second Street, then swing back west. Head on home."

"I want to call Ben."

"Not from here, Jake!" Rickie's voice had lost its smooth, soothing sound. "Use a pay phone on the way. Try Lex. There's actually one over there that works. I made a call the other night. Around Ninety-third Street,

I think. And call 911, not Ben! I don't even like you phoning from Carnegie Hill, but you can't risk taking a cab or bus downtown. Just give the operator the bare facts—there's a body in Tony Silva's house—then hang up. Now, let's move it!"

Modesty and I watched in awe as Rickie slipped out the window and rappelled down into the dark alley.

Our own exit, while far less treacherous, proved to be no less terrifying. Once in the foyer, we froze. Stood on that marble floor, like statues. My hand on the door knob, but incapable of turning it.

Modesty finally spoke. "Remember *The Lady or the Tiger*? Who knows what's waiting on the other side of the door? That patrol car could be parked out front!"

A surge of adrenaline, masquerading as courage, emboldened me. "I'm going first. The cops would recognize you. I can pass as a resident who, realizing her dog's gone missing, is heading out to find him!" Before she could stop me—it wouldn't have taken much—I yanked the heavy door open and stepped out on the stoop.

Only the still of the night greeted me. Flustered, for a moment, I couldn't recall if I should go left or right. Some second-story woman I'd make. Then, following Rickie's instructions, I turned toward Fifth, waving my doggie poop bag in front of me like a badge of honor.

Walking up Fifth, I said "Hi" in response to a doorman's greeting. Damn glad to see a live, friendly face. In this costume, no need to worry about him being able to ID me in some future lineup. Going east on 95th, I saw three taxis, two homeless ladies, and one drunk. An old guy. No one paid any attention to me.

Lots of action going down on Lexington. Stragglers weaving their way home, after last calls at local bars. Workers, leaving late shifts, heading for the subway. People walking real dogs. Not a cop in sight. I felt safe.

And, as promised, a pay phone. I stepped into the cubicle, dialed 911, and blurted out my murder. As soon the operator started asking questions, I hung up.

I smelled him before I saw him. Or even sensed someone behind me. Breathing hot, rancid air on my left cheek.

Pure panic swept over me.

"Something wrong, lady?" Gruff. Taunting.

Slowly, I turned around. His uniform hat, literally, in my face. Boy, the NYPD kept shrinking every day.

"Is there a problem, Officer?" I knew how silly I looked in the wig and glasses.

"You tell me, lady." A Bronx accent. A Fort Apache attitude. A face even a mother might have serious trouble loving. "Didja jest report a moider?"

My mind mush, everything a jumble. Had I given 911 the address first? Then reported the murder? Then smelled him? If so, could I bluff my way out of this?

I could damn well try. "It's my baby, Officer! Totsie." I stuck the doggie poop bag up under his nose. "The most beautiful white poodle that you ever saw! She's run away and I've had a vision. Totsie's been murdered! I just called 911. I can't believe how quickly you got here! You have to help me find her body. I think it's in the Cloisters!"

He backed away, shaking his head.

I was home free!

Thirty-one

I arrived at the house just before three—ending what had to have been the fastest, yet longest, hour of my life. Before embarking on this caper I'd turned off my cell phone and stashed it in my sock. Now I locked the lobby door, stepped into the elevator, retrieved the phone, and listened to my two messages.

"Jake, this is Dennis. I know you're up to no good, but it's after midnight. Shouldn't you be getting your beauty sleep? I'm giving you the luxury of a few more hours of rest. We're going to the Hamptons by helicopter. Meet me at the Fifty-ninth Street Heliport at nine. We should be back in the city before noon. I'd pick you up, but I'm having breakfast at the Plaza with Greg Ford. So I'll see you over at the East River. Unless, of course, you wind up in jail tonight. In that case, take two aspirins and call me in the morning. I'll recommend a clever criminal attorney."

The second message was from Too Tall Tom.

"You're never going to believe this! It's eleven-thirty!

*Where are you? Out on the town with Modesty, doing
some detective work without me? Well, I'll just bet you
two can't top what I've been up to! Darling, I've had a
Dashiell Hammett evening! Too bad you couldn't have
been with me, playing Lillian Hellman!"*

When I reached the second floor, I kept listening, hoping this wouldn't be one of his famous fifteen-minute
messages.

*"Ms. Sharpe-Fielding had me working overtime. No
time and a half, I assure you! Anyway, I just finished
staining the master bedroom cornice this deadly shade
of aquamarine—think of that absolutely ghastly blue-
green tile, so overused, in 1950s bathrooms."*

God, would he ever get to the point?

*"The phone rang around ten-thirty. Rebecca, who was
in the bedroom with me, barking out orders, answered
it. I heard her say, 'You know you can't come here. No!
That's out of the question!' I tell you, Jake, she turned
purple. An even uglier color than the cornice. Then she
said, 'I think you're crazy. He said what? Goddamn!
Okay, in ten minutes.' She slammed down the receiver
and turned to me. 'Go home, we'll pick up from here in
the morning!' I left, but I didn't go home. I walked
across Fifth Avenue and waited on a park bench. Sure
enough, not ten minutes later, a taxi pulled up and—of
all the people in all the world—guess who jumped out?
Tony Silva! Now am I a shaman or what? And a good
citizen! I immediately reported his visit to Ben Rubin.
Ciao! Call me!"*

God! There you go! So much for Modesty's, Rickie's,
and my investigative conclusions! Tony Silva hadn't
been murdered in his mansion. Or fled the country either. As of ten-forty this evening, he'd been only a few
blocks away, very much alive, calling on his long-
rumored mistress, Rebecca Sharpe-Fielding. I'd think

about this tomorrow. Right now I had to go to bed.

Gypsy Rose sat in the living room, watching a video-tape of *Ghost*. "I couldn't sleep, Jake. Damn, Whoopi's good, isn't she?"

"Thanks for staying with Mom." I kissed her well-creamed cheek. "Why couldn't you sleep?" I yearned for bed.

"Worrying about Maura. Thank God, Aaron's taking her to the funeral. I've got to get back to the bookstore!" She sighed. "And worrying about you. That's quite a get-up you've got on, Jake!"

Damn! I yanked off the Morticia wig and the glasses. "Kind of hard to explain . . ."

"Darling, you look exhausted, Go to bed."

"There's something else, isn't there?"

Gypsy Rose laughed. "Who's the psychic here? But, yes, there is. In addition to worrying about my friends here on earth, my friends from the world beyond keep dropping into my dreams. I know they're trying to send a message, but I don't get it. I think they're trying to warn us. Be careful, Jake. I sense that where you're go-ing tomorrow could be dangerous. Agnes Scanlon's. Right?"

"Did Dennis tell you that?"

"Not exactly." She smiled. "He merely confirmed it. Jake, the poor guy has called three times. Talk about worried. Did you get his message? He left one on your cell phone."

"Yes. Dennis is flying me out to the Hamptons to see Aunt Agnes. I'm meeting him at the heliport in the morning."

"Good. I'm glad you're not driving."

Knowing I'd be sorry, I asked, "Why?"

"Well, you see, St. Thomas More showed up in my dreams. Along with Zelda and Dashell Hammett. A first for him, though Lillian's been around before. St. Thomas seemed all worked up about a car . . . fretting over . . . no . . . I can't see it clearly, but . . ."

"Don't even try, Gypsy Rose. Let's just go to bed."

"Maybe I can get some rest now that you're home, Jake." She ejected *Ghost*. "And a few hours' sleep might bring us to a brighter day."

. . . . .

Thunder and lightning jarred me awake thirty minutes before the alarm was set to go off. So much for a brighter day. With only four and a half hours of sleep, I still felt weary. I rolled over.

. . . . .

I knew I was dreaming, but couldn't will myself awake. Tony Silva kissed me one last time, then hopped out of bed to get us something to drink. My long dark hair, matted with sweat, covered the pillow. I felt happy. Sated. Could I be in love with Tony? This certainly felt like love. I shut my eyes. Then I heard the rustle of a sheet, raised my head, and stared into the barrel of a gun. "Karen!" I turned toward the door. Tony stood there, naked, holding two small, glass bottles of Coca-Cola. The caps removed. He ran toward the bed. A flash of blue caught my attention as the killer spun around to face Tony, then quickly turned back to me and pulled the trigger.

. . . . .

I woke up. Shaking. Soaking wet. Jesus! That blue shirt had been worn by someone else. The alarm blared. The phone rang. I grabbed the receiver. Just another day in Carnegie Hill.

"Jake, you certainly were on target about this case," Ben said. Not according to my most recent dream. "So, be careful. Two more people are dead and every cop in the city, plus the FBI, are out looking for Tony Silva!"

Better late than never, I thought. Then what he'd said sunk in. "Did you say two more people are dead?"

"Yeah. Someone made an anonymous call to 911 from a phone booth on Lexington. We found Clare Blake's body in Tony's mansion." Did Ben suspect who that "someone" might be? "Then Too Tall Tom called me last night. Has he told you about what he overheard at Rebecca Sharpe-Fielding's?"

"He left me a message." Why had I said that? Now Ben would know I'd been out last night!

"Well, when we arrived at her place, Tony had gone. The doorman said he'd only been upstairs for a few minutes. And . . ."

"And what?"

"He'd shot Rebecca in the head. She's dead, too, Jake."

"Oh, God!"

"Dad's on his way over there now. He'll take Maura to the funeral. Don't worry, he won't let your mother out of his sight. And the FBI is watching her. Stay put, Jake. Don't go anywhere! Let Homicide work this one. I don't want anything to happen to you."

"Um," I said, thinking about my upcoming helicopter ride.

"And, Jake, when this is over, we have to talk."

"We do?" My heart took yet another nosedive.

"Look, I have to go . . . but . . . well . . . for God's sake, you do know how much I love you, don't you?"

My mother flung my bedroom door open. "Jake, Aaron's here. Clare Blake is dead!"

I nodded at her and said, "Ben?"

He'd hung up.

Thirty-two

I'd never ridden in a helicopter. Thank God, the thunder and lightning had stopped. As I walked to the runway, the wind factor alarmed me, but both Dennis and the pilot sported big, confident grins.

"Say hello to Mike Garson," Dennis said.

I shook Mike's hand, thinking that he looked like a high school kid. Freckled face, skinny, dressed in denim cutoffs and a white T-shirt, his carrot hair hidden under a baseball cap. How old did you have to be to get a license to fly one of these things?

Dennis, on the other hand, wore a Brooks Brothers summer twill suit, a Turnbull & Asser shirt, and Bruno Magli loafers. I'd wager that his outfit cost more than my entire summer wardrobe. Hell, probably, more than three years' worth of summer wardrobes.

We climbed on board. I pulled my seat belt as tight as I could and squeezed Dennis's hand even tighter.

"Relax," he said, as we whirled straight up in the air.

I could barely hear him over the roar of the motor. This time my stomach, not my heart, lurched.

He pointed downtown. "Look, there's the Chrysler Building." I ventured a peek out my window. We were level with its scalloped steeple, but flying lower than the Empire State Building's observation deck. I could picture *King Kong* reaching out and grabbing hold of that airplane.

By the time we passed over Rockaway Beach, I began to enjoy myself. An awesome Atlantic Ocean down below and fluffy white clouds and yards of blue sky right outside our windows. Too cool! My mood soared from *King Kong* to *Jonathan Livingston Seagull*.

I never noticed how pensive Dennis had become until we landed at the East Hampton airport. Other than thanking Mike, telling him we'd be back in a hour or so, and arranging for a cab to take us to Dune Road, he'd hardly spoken.

Once we were settled in the taxi, I asked, "What's wrong, Dennis?"

He shrugged. "I wish I knew. Have you heard about Clare Blake and Rebecca?"

"Yes. Ben called early this morning. How do you know? Was it on the news?"

"Not on the program that I listened to, but then I left the house early. Greg Ford told me during breakfast." He shook his head. "Strange man, that Ford."

"Strange group of friends," I said. "Does Greg think Tony Silva killed both of them?"

"Well, who else could have done it?" Dennis stared hard at me as if he believed I had the answer.

The driver made a sudden turn, pulling into a long, winding driveway, and said, "This is it, folks." The approach to the Tara-like white house, set back on a field of green grass, included a view of the beach and the ocean. Quite a backyard.

We asked the driver to wait and walked up to the front door. Dennis rapped three times, like a man on a mission.

A small, dark-haired, middle-aged woman in a nurse's uniform opened the door.

"Yes." Polite puzzlement in her tone. Total rejection in her body language.

"I'm Jake O'Hara. Could you please tell Miss Scanlon I'd like to speak to her?" The woman frowned and made a move to shut the door. I begged, "Just for a few minutes."

"I'm sorry, Miss Scanlon is very ill. She receives no visitors, other than her physician." As the door swung shut, I pushed it back open. "Well, she'll see me. Tell her I'm a friend of her late niece, Karen, and I have some information regarding her murder. Mr. Kim is my attorney."

Looking unsure, the nurse ushered us in. "Please have a seat in the parlor." She pointed to a small, rather formal room off the impressive center hall. "I'll tell Miss Scanlon you're here."

"So you're Karen's friend and I'm your attorney." Dennis chuckled. "What tales of fiction you do spin, Ms. Ghostwriter O'Hara. Let's hope old Aunt Agnes is too feeble to do the math. Since you were born on the day that Karen died, even a creative mind like yours might be hard pressed to explain your 'friendship' with a dead woman."

"Shush!" I spotted the white uniform in the doorway.

"Follow me, please," the nurse said, "Miss Scanlon is waiting for you on the sun porch."

Sitting in a peacock rattan chair straight out of *A Passage to India*, Aunt Agnes looked more like Queen Victoria, in the heyday of the British Empire, than the sick old lady I'd expected. Same hair style, parted in the middle and pulled back in a bun. Same lace collar, worn over a navy blue voile ankle-length dress. Same imperious manner.

She stared at Dennis and me with complete disdain. Then allowing a hint of a smile, said, "I've been waiting for you to show up for thirty-four years."

What a hook! I've never written a better opening line!

I introduced Dennis and myself, then asked, "Miss Scanlon, why did you say that? Who do you think we are?"

"Hell, I have no idea who you are!" She might be sick, but her voice sounded strong and her shrewd eyes met mine boldly. "But you told Nurse Crachet that you had information regarding Karen's murder. In all this time, no one has contacted me directly. I figured you must be connected to the money. Aren't you?"

Damn. What money? Could she be senile? I didn't think so. Not this sly old fox. I kept quiet—betting that she wouldn't. Dennis, as an attorney, knew when to remain silent. He contemplated his expensive shoes. I counted to thirty.

Aunt Agnes spoke. "So, tell me, Jake O'Hara, who set me up with more than 100,000 dollars of income, every year since Karen died?"

"Is that how you bought this house?"

She snapped, "Are you daft? Or are you playing games with me? I saved for a few years, then bought. How else would a cleaning woman from the bowels of South Jersey end up on the beach in Southampton? I'm dying, you know, and, like Pip in *Great Expectations*, I just want to find out who my benefactor is."

"I'm sorry." I meant it. Aunt Agnes was one feisty lady.

"Lungs. Gave out after sixty years of smoking!" She gestured to the round rattan table next to her. A half-empty pack of Chesterfields lay next to a black and white photograph in a silver frame. "Since I've already killed myself, I'll just keep putting another nail in my coffin." She reached for her cigarettes.

Dennis said, "Do you think . . . should you be . . . smoking?"

"You're far too young to tell me what to do," she said. "And far too young to have drawn up my trust fund. Do you know who did?"

I never heard his answer. I'd picked up the photograph and was staring into the faces of five good-looking young people. A smiling Karen in the middle, flanked by Andy and Rebecca on her right and Greg on her left. Next to Greg, with an arm draped around his shoulder, stood the handsome, young man of my dreams. Tony Silva!

So, they had all known one another! And both the Fieldings and Greg Ford had lied to the police!

Inside my head, like a movie, frame by frame, plot points unfolded, clues added up, motive and money commingled, and a cover-up became clear. Before the final scene, I knew who'd killed Karen.

Thirty-three

"A conspiracy theory!" Dennis bellowed. "Involving the U.S. Attorney?" Not wanting to get sand in his shoes, he was hopping on one foot, trying to remove his loafer and sock.

When we'd left Aunt Agnes, happily lighting up another cigarette, I'd dragged him out on the beach for this chat, not wanting to discuss my denouement in the taxi. Since I'd worn chinos and Nikes, I had no concerns about sand or surf.

A gust of wind blew strands of hair in my eyes. The whitecaps dancing atop big, dark blue waves made me think another storm might be coming. "Why don't you just listen first, then get upset? It will save time."

He grinned. "Logic. One of the many reasons why I love you, Jake!" He brushed my hair away and kissed my forehead. "Shoot."

We both laughed. I took a deep breath. This wouldn't be an easy sell. "Okay, but hear me out, before rushing to judgment!"

Now barefoot, he placed his shoes on a dune, then gave me his full attention. "Agreed."

"Tony Silva didn't shoot Karen, Greg Ford did."

Dennis started, but true to his word, kept his counsel. I hesitated, knowing that several of my conclusions had been based on dreams, not facts.

"Tony had gone into the kitchen. Ford used a key, or Karen hadn't locked the door, but he came there with a gun. And Tony caught him in the act of killing Karen. Think about it. A poor guy, at George Washington on scholarship, who needed money. Maybe Tony blackmailed Greg. Or Greg bribed him. Either way, Ford paid Tony's tuition at NYU and all his expenses. Including that apartment on Broome. How else could Silva have stayed here? And Greg had enough cash on hand to bribe a bunch of people, right?"

Dennis asked, "Do I have permission to speak?"

I kissed his cheek. "Granted."

"Barrels of dough. By eighteen, he'd inherited huge trust funds from both his deceased mother and his paternal grandfather. His mother's alone totaled over twenty million. In 1960s dollars."

"Okay. So after he'd bought Tony's silence, he bought an alibi from his good friends, Andy and Rebecca. I'll bet they never knew that he killed Karen. He probably said he'd been at her apartment, but if the police found out, they'd drag the Ford family name through the mud. If they'd swear he'd been with them, they'd be set for life. It would have been convenient for them to believe him. Made the cover-up more palatable. And think of the perks. Andy could attend Harvard Law with Greg, mingle with his friends, meet the people who'd get him started in politics. Rebecca would never have to go home again. She'd receive her MBA and her Ph.D., and Greg would introduce her to the right crowd.

His Wall Street and banking connections, who'd mentor her career in finance."

"Sounds like a B movie," Dennis said.

"Doesn't it ever?"

"Then what?"

"Well, as with any scenerio, there's a lot of what ifs." I sighed. "For example, what if Tony, either at Greg's suggestion or through a direct approach from Cali, had become the American front man for the Mexican drug cartel? Or what if Rebecca's Latin contacts—and her laundering of Mexican drug money—had led Tony to his position as lobbyist for the Intra-American Trade Assocation? We'll have to check out which of those 'business arrangements' came first. However, a lobbyist as cover for a career as the United States Attorney's hit man is a great plot twist, isn't it? We can be certain that Andy Fielding's winding up as chair of the House Foreign Relations Committee was no coincidence. And what about this: Greg Ford is the master mind behind the whole enchilada."

"So Tony Silva killed Father Blake on Ford's orders? Because of Nick Amas's confession. And Father Blake's manuscript." Spoken like a man who almost bought into my theory.

"Right! Amas had taken his orders from Silva. Ford believed Amas implicated Silva during that confession. Tony's working for Greg placed the United States Attorney at high risk of exposure. A strong motive, wouldn't you say? And Ford, being a WASP, probably, wouldn't have trusted Blake to keep his vow of silence."

"What if Blake knew Greg had killed Karen, but for all those years, could never reveal his awful secret?" I loved it! Dennis was playing what if with me! "Silva might have gone to confession after having witnessing the murder and agreeing to the cover-up."

"Yes! When Silva shot Father Blake, he'd snuffed out two secrets with one bullet, hadn't he? Then poor Clare, convinced her brother had been killed for what he knew about a thirty-four-year-old murder, started nosing around, and Tony killed her, too!"

"And Rebecca?"

"Well, what if she finally woke up and counted the bodies? Maybe, she'd realized that Greg and Tony were killers and became a threat to them. God, do you think Andy's next?" I suddenly felt faint—again. "Come on, Dennis, let's get back to New York. Now! My mother's at a funeral with a man who wants her dead!"

Thirty-four

The wind that had propelled us forward on the flight out whipped us around on the way back. We thanked Mike and hopped off, greeted by a pelting rain. Dennis had arranged for a limo to meet us in front of the heliport. The driver greeted us with a huge umbrella.

Ten past noon. Father Blake's funeral had started at eleven. Allowing for eulogies and a church full of communicants, the service should run to 12:30. I asked the driver to hurry.

"Lady, this is midday Manhattan. You're going up, then crosstown. Whattaya want, a miracle?"

I did. But, as noted, we weren't in Lourdes, and the FDR Drive remained bumper to bumper.

Dennis raised the plastic shield that separated us from the driver. "Listen, Jake, your scenario has more than a few holes and not a hell of a lot of facts, but I think you're right. Try not to worry. Your mother's with Aaron, I'm sure she's safe. At the moment, I'm more concerned about how we can prove any of this."

I suspected he was using a diversionary tactic here—getting my mind back on the case and off my mother's proximity to a multiple murderer.

But I had an answer. "Remember that message from Don Taylor that Zelda delivered to you during the seance? I bet we'll find Karen's portrait in Greg Ford's home—and Father Blake's missing manuscript will be in the safe behind it!"

Dennis groaned.

"Hey, you know, Gypsy Rose's seances have a more than fifty percent success rate." Of course, I'd just made up that statistic. I kissed, then bit his hand. Gently.

"Let's go to Venice. We can be married in St. Mark's. Fly everyone over. They can stay at Cipriani's."

"Dennis!" I pictured myself drifting in a gondola, ribbons in my hair. Like Katharine Hepburn. Very cool.

"Think about it. You could beat your mother down the aisle."

He knew me too well. "Watch out, I might say yes."

"Except for Ben Rubin?"

"No. Yes. No."

He grinned. "Well, we'll always have Carnegie Hill."

I burst out laughing. My feet tingled. Then I shocked myself. "You're so easy to love, Dennis Kim. Can I give you my answer tomorrow?"

He hummed the theme from *Summertime*.

My cell phone rang. Too Tall Tom. "You never called me back!"

"Sorry. I've been *really* busy."

"Well, since my client's been murdered, I thought you might have some other detective work for me to do."

"Where are you?"

"At Sarabeth's with Modesty."

"Good! Run down to St. Thomas More's and find my mother. Dennis and I are trying to get there, but we're stuck in traffic. Keep Mom away from Greg Ford!"

"My God, do you mean . . ."

"Please go! Now!" I hung up.

· · · · ·

We reached the church at 12:35. The funeral cortège, parked out front, could be a good sign. With Clare gone, Father Blake's fellow priests were his only family. And they were still inside. Maybe Mom was, too.

"Jake!" Mrs. McMahon, dressed in full funeral regalia, stood under a big, black umbrella. So she'd been included on the invitation list. That had to have made her day. Made her year.

"Hello, Mrs. McMahon. Do you know where my mother is?"

"Such a beautiful service. Why, the cardinal—"

I screamed, "Have you seen my mother?"

"No need to raise your voice, Jake O'Hara. And in front of God's house! Yes, I've seen your mother. She left a few minutes ago with her boyfriend and some younger man. They drove away in a fancy, foreign car."

"What did the other man look like?" I could hear the hysteria in my voice.

"Let me think . . . he did look familiar. I know! He reminded me of John Wayne."

Dennis caught me before I fell to the ground.

Too Tall Tom dashed out of the church, Modesty scurrying behind him. "Your mother's nowhere to be found!"

"Where's Ben Rubin?" Dennis punched in 911 on his cell phone.

Too Tall Tom said, "Talking to Andrew Fielding in the back of the church. I overheard him ask the widower to drop by the Nineteenth Precinct this afternoon. Think Andy hired Silva to bump off Rebecca?"

"No! The killer just kidnapped Mom."

Mrs. McMahon clutched my arm, "Your mother's boyfriend? Our former DA murdered that congressman's wife?"

I yanked her hand off my dripping shirt. "Not Aaron Rubin, you twit! Greg Ford."

A breathless Ben Rubin came running up to us, waving his cell phone. "Jake! I'm talking to your mother. She and Dad are locked in the trunk of Greg Ford's Mercedes." He raced toward his unmarked police car, parked across the street. Dennis and I, right behind him, jumped into the back seat.

Modesty and Too Tall Tom commandeered the flower car. As we roared off toward Madison, I heard its driver shouting, "Stop! That's the property of Kearn's Funeral Home!"

Ben, radioing for backup, tossed his cell phone to Dennis. "Press the speaker button. See if she knows which way they're going!"

Ben barked out instructions. "Black Mercedes. Registered to Greg Ford. Yes, that Greg Ford. Last seen heading west from Eighty-ninth Street between Park and Madison."

"Maura, this is Dennis. Jake and I are with Ben. Hang on! We're coming. Do you have any idea where you are?"

"Thank God!" Eerie. Mom's voice came through loud and clear, almost as if she were sitting next to me. "Okay, here's what I do know. Greg had his driver cut through the park. Heading to the West Side. While we were in one of those stone tunnels, the driver turned around, and pointed a gun at us."

Ben reported, "They went through Central Park. Probably used the Eighty-sixth Street entrance."

"Tony Silva," Dennis said.

"Right. Then he and Greg made us get out of the car, and ordered us to climb into the trunk. Aaron tried to take the gun away from Tony." Mom's voice broke. "That murdering bastard hit Aaron so hard, he passed out. Then they tossed him in the trunk and made me crawl in after him."

I grabbed the phone from Dennis. "Mom, is Aaron okay?"

"Unconscious, but breathing regularly." She sighed. "I love you, Jake. Be careful." Sobbing, I handed the phone back to Dennis.

We turned left on Fifth, Ben weaving through the traffic, his siren blaring.

As we made the right turn into the park, two patrol cars arrived, pulling in front of the flower car. I could imagine Modesty's reaction to that. Our little caravan headed west.

Mom said, "We've just veered right. Silva spun around so fast, I shifted from one side of the trunk to the other. I hope I didn't hurt Aaron."

God! Mom sounded so calm. So brave. I cursed myself for sometimes categorizing her as frivolous fluff.

Ben ordered police cars onto every northbound avenue on the West Side.

I said, "Where are they?" God! They could have turned right on Central Park West or on the West Side Highway. Or on any number of uptown avenues in between!

Dennis asked Mom, "Maura, can you estimate how much time elapsed from when you climbed into the trunk to Tony's right turn?"

"No. God, no I can't. But I pressed Ben's number right after they closed the lid. Greg had grabbed my bag and Aaron's cell phone. Good thing I had mine in my pants pocket."

Ben said, "Enough time for me to make an educated guess. The highway. Probably heading for the bridge."

Lots of static came from Ben's two-way radio, followed by, "We have the cell phone signal. The West Side Highway, around Ninety-eighth Street."

Ben said, "On our way!"

No car chase in any movie had ever been as nerve-racking as this, the real thing! With the siren blasting, Ben drove west, darting between cars and dodging pedestrians. When we reached the highway, a motorcycle cop had halted all northbound traffic to 96th Street. Drivers and passengers rubbernecked and bellyached, but remained immobile. With no cars to impede him, Ben really pumped that pedal. I couldn't check the speedometer, but I'd bet we were going 90 miles an hour.

Ben yelled, "There he is!"

"We're on your tail, Maura," Dennis said, "hang on!"

Above 96th Street, most of the cars had merged into one line, knowing a madman was among them. Once Tony spotted us, he raised the stakes to well over 100, careening dangerously, banging into bumpers and sideswiping any car in his path.

I screamed, "Jesus! He'll kill them all!"

My mother said, "I'm frightened, Dennis. We're going so fast . . . poor Aaron. I'm holding his head. Oh God!"

I watched as the Mercedes flew up and over the cement divider, popping open the trunk door, sending Mom and Aaron sprawling out onto the West Side Highway, before it crashed headlong into a southbound SUV.

Epilogue

Thursday evening. Seven P.M.

My mother, propped up in bed in Columbia Presbyterian Hospital, had her left arm in a cast, her right in a sling, a badly bruised chin, and a smile on her face. Most of Mom had landed on top of Aaron, but she'd flung her arms out in front of her and they'd taken the brunt of the damage.

She asked, "And you're certain that Aaron's going to be okay?"

I laughed. "For the third time, yes."

Gypsy Rose, who'd just arrived with pot roast and roses, said, "He has a concussion, doesn't he? Dennis told me that when he called."

"Yes. Tony really whacked him. And when he tumbled out of the trunk, he sprained an ankle and scraped his face." I smiled. "Then Mom landed on him! But the doctor said he'll recover fully."

Gypsy Rose sighed. "I told you a car—"

"You are so psychic!" I kissed her cheek.

"Where are Modesty and Too Tall Tom?"

"Returning that flower car they *borrowed* to an irate undertaker."

She smiled. "And Dennis?"

"He's sitting with Aaron," I said. "As you can imagine, Ben's been busy."

Tony Silva had gone through the windshield. No seat belt. He'd been DOA when he arrived in the ER. Ben had cuffed a seriously banged up, but ambulatory, United States Attorney. Sandy Ellis had read Congressman Andrew Fielding his Miranda rights, then booked him on conspiracy charges. Just for starters. How much he'd actually known about the murders of Karen Scanlon, Father Blake, Don Taylor, Clare Blake, and his wife, Rebecca Sharpe-Fielding, remains, for the moment, a mystery. However, he hired Johnnie Cochran to represent him. Senor Cali, still professing that he was only an innocent international businessman, had also been taken into custody.

When Ben searched Greg's Dakota apartment, he found documents linking Rebecca and Andy to the drug cartel. And a memo from Rebecca—probably her death warrant—hinting she suspected Ford had a direct connection to Father Blake's death.

The priest's manuscript had been hidden in a safe behind a portrait of Karen Scanlon. Ford had tucked a lock of dark hair into the frame. Gypsy Rose had batted a psychic home run.

Suddenly, I felt like a new woman. Or, maybe, my old self. With my own soul. Sensing I wouldn't be seeing Karen in my dreams, I decided to go to Calvary tomorrow and say good-bye to her.

I smiled, recalling Dennis's proposal. And my promise to make a decision.

Don't stop thinking about tomorrow . . .

Miriam Grace Monfredo

brings to life one of the most exciting periods in our nation's history—the mid-1800s—when the passionate struggles of suffragettes, abolitionists, and other heroes touched the lives of every American, including a small-town librarian named Glynis Tryon...

__**BLACKWATER SPIRITS**   0-425-15266-9/$6.50

Glynis Tryon, no stranger to political controversy, is fighting the prejudice against the Seneca Iroquois. And the issue becomes personal when one of Glynis's Iroquois friends is accused of murder...

__**NORTH STAR CONSPIRACY**   0-425-14720-7/$6.50

__**SENECA FALLS INHERITANCE**

0-425-14465-8/$6.99

__**THROUGH A GOLD EAGLE**   0-425-15898-5/$6.50

When abolitionist John Brown is suspected of moving counterfeit bills, Glynis is compelled to launch her own campaign for freedom—to free an innocent man.

BETSY DEVONSHIRE NEEDLECRAFT MYSTERIES
by Monica Ferris

FREE NEEDLEWORK PATTERN INCLUDED IN EACH MYSTERY!

❑ **CREWEL WORLD**

0-425-16780-1/$5.99

When Betsy's sister is murdered in her own needlework store, Betsy takes over the shop and the investigation. But to find the murderer, she'll have to put together a list of motives and suspects to figure out the killer's pattern of crime...

❑ **FRAMED IN LACE**

0-425-17149-3/$5.99

A skeleton is discovered when the historic Hopkins ferry is raised from the lake. Unfortunately, the only evidence found was a piece of lace-like fabric. But once Betsy and the patrons of the needlecraft shop lend a hand, they're sure to stitch together this mystery...

❑ **A STITCH IN TIME**

0-425-17149-3/$5.99

A skeleton is discovered when the historic Hopkins ferry is raised from the lake. Unfortunately, the only evidence found was a piece of lace-like fabric. But once Betsy and the patrons of the needlecraft shop lend a hand, they're sure to stitch together this mystery...